UZZIAH MEETS THE PROPHET

UZZIAH MEETS THE PROPHET

A WESTERN DOUBLE

UZZIAH MOUNTAIN MAN
BOOK SIX

J.J. BONHAM

Uzziah Meets the Prophet: A Western Double
Paperback Edition

Wolfpack Publishing
1707 E. Diana Street
Tampa, FL 33610

www.wolfpackpublishing.com

Paperback ISBN 979-8-89567-803-9
Ebook ISBN 979-8-89567-802-2

UZZIAH MEETS THE PROPHET

UZZIAH MEETS THE PROPHET

1

Riding a trail north beside the Mississippi wasn't the safest place to be in this old world, but as far as Uzziah was concerned, he could have cared less. The last few months, first being incarcerated and the trial in which they were not convicted but released, seemed to bode nothing but good for the two mountain men. Then they were thrown that curveball by Patrick Gass, and Immanuel, immediately accepting the offer to travel south to a city as large as Baltimore, 102,000 people. Well, Uzziah would have taken the time to think about that one, but Immanuel hadn't allowed him the opportunity.

He realized he had been a crutch to Immanuel in his drinking, after all, he did carry a bottle of whiskey with him at all times. The original reason for that had been as an antiseptic. Alcohol would clean a wound and keep infection away until you could reach a doctor, not to mention its ability to render a man accepting of things that could happen to him that he wouldn't normally allow. And yet, even when he knew that

Immanuel was drinking too much and smoking too much, the man had a bear-sized cough on him, and his color hadn't been good recently, he still didn't step in and say anything. Until they had been confined indoors for what seemed years, and it had only been two and a half months. Immanuel's tan had diminished, and Uzziah could see the unhealthy skin tone of the man beneath the hue that the sun had put on him. He hadn't thought much about it. But that had certainly changed.

In fact, it wasn't until they got back to their hotel room the night Immanuel tried to pick up on Edgar Allan Poe's Virginia, that they had finally discussed the very things he'd been concerned about.

"We don't need to go to no New Orleans," Uzziah had emphatically said.

"Why are ya doin' this, huh? It's the opportunity of a lifetime, partner, can't ya see that?"

"All I see is more drinking, more whoring, and the such," Uzziah came back.

"As I said, the opportunity of a lifetime, U," he only called him *U* when he wanted Uzziah to feel that they were the best of friends, and they were, but Uzziah did not like to be manipulated, and it felt like Immanuel had made up his mind before considering Uzziah's mindset, and Uzziah didn't like that.

"I came out with ya to the Rockies to learn to be a mountain man," Uzziah said.

"And I dern near taught ya all ya need to know."

"Ain't no mountain men in Louisiana, Immanuel, and ya know it."

"Well, guess what, there will be, when we get there!" he said and slapped Uzziah on the back.

That was the end of the discussion, Immanuel still

felt, in his heart of hearts, that he was the boss in the partnership. That would have been fine with Uzziah, five or six years ago, but like with most things that the young man from Virginia ran into in the mountains, he already had a plan for what to do, before Immanuel said what to do. In fact, their actions and prompt reactions were generally the same. Uzziah was confident in his abilities and knew when he got back to the cabins, he could fix them and take care of himself.

Of course, there was the matter of it being nearly fall, and he would be back way too late to prepare for a mountain winter. That being said, he thought if he was going to tell Benjamin's mother, Loretta Stevens—he thought he remembered her name right—that he died like a hero, then he'd probably be going to Columbus, Ohio first, then most likely go see his family in the Shenandoah Valley. Rahab, his ma, would be thrilled to have him back, and his pa, Sean, would, too. Not to mention the passal of brothers and sisters that he surely loved. He could spend the winter there, then take off in the summer for the Rockies.

"Hold it there, mister!" a voice came out of the darkness.

Well, thought Uzziah, he'd sure bungled up this ride, thinking with his head in the clouds when he should have been watching his backtrail, but these three very dirty gents were standing in the middle of the dirt road right in front of him.

Uzziah started to say something that might forgo violence, but Jenny had stopped on the backtrail—probably eating some weeds or something—and now she was out of the brush to Uzziah's right, and she brayed as loud as she ever had!

"What the—" the one holding the gun on Uzziah said, and well, he'd turned his head and the old flintlock pistol toward Jenny, so...

"Boom!" the Hawken roared, and the man who had been standing there with the gun was thrown back about three feet, and he had a very large hole where his heart had been.

The other two started scrambling for their weapons, and Uzziah impaled the one nearest Jenny with his Bowie and planted a tomahawk into the skull of the last one, who stood there, looking up at the wooden handle of the tomahawk like he was wondering what had just happened.

Both the one impaled by the Bowie and the tomahawked one dropped at about the same time. Jenny braying all the while.

"Girl, I am so glad ya come along, when we get to Virginia I'ma feed you oats till they come out yer ears," Uzziah said as he stroked her under the chin, and she raised her head like she was saying, *Please don't stop*!

He put his boot heel on the knifed one and pulled it out, wiping the blade on the man's dirty shirt, he wasn't sure whether it made the blade any cleaner, but it took the blood off it. He'd have to remember to clean it before he ate with it, since most meals were eaten with the big knife.

The young man with the tomahawk in his forehead wasn't quite dead, and when Uzziah grabbed the mean-looking weapon and was about to jerk it from the man's skull, he spoke up.

"We didn't mean ya no harm," he said as clear as day.

"Whatcha doin' out on the road pullin' guns on people?" Uzziah asked him.

"We didn't mean ya no harm," he said again, still as clear as day with his speech.

"What's yer name?" Uzziah asked him, squatting down next to him.

"We didn't mean ya no harm," he said again.

Well, that wasn't exactly true, and it seemed the man's speech was limited to the one lie, so Uzziah stood, put his boot on the man's head, and jerked the tomahawk from his skull.

The young man's head was opened up, and bleeding badly as he jumped up and ran down the road north. There was some moon out, but Uzziah lost him as he'd run out of seeing range.

Uzziah stood there and scratched his head. He'd never seen anything like that. A man with a deadly wound running down a road, he wondered if he'd see his body later in the night. Perhaps he should have shot the young man in the back as he was running away, but somehow it just didn't seem fair. Immanuel probably would have, just to end the mystery, but Uzziah wasn't going to do that. Who knew, maybe the man would run home, get patched up, and live the rest of his life, telling people, *We didn't mean ya no harm.*

Uzziah took Shadow and Jenny off the road and traveled in the woods for a couple of hours, just in case there were more bandits who might be a bit more skillful. At one point, not long after he was traveling through the woods north, he heard voices. He tied Shadow up and asked him to keep Jenny quiet, it was a job that he was actually good at.

He walked over toward the direction of the road,

and the young man he'd tomahawked was lying in the road, muttering to no one in particular. Uzziah wondered if he was in any pain and decided he might be. He certainly wouldn't let an animal go down like that, so he stepped out onto the road, looking about, making sure no one was nearby. The young man was still perfecting his one and only sentence about not meaning harm. Uzziah took the razor-sharp Bowie and slit the boy's throat. He placed his hand over the boy's heart and could feel it beating weaker and weaker, till it stopped. He reached down, closed the boy's eyes, and dragged him off the road, but not too far, in case kin came looking.

The false dawn came weakly through the trees, and Uzziah decided to get back on the road, he'd make better time. He wasn't sure where he was, although he knew the last bit of town they'd seen had been Cairo, Illinois, where the confluence of the Ohio River meets the Mississippi.

It wasn't much of a town until the Cairo City and Canal Company built a large levee around the city. Still, that wasn't far. He thought about it for a moment, and it seemed they had traveled less than a day by the time he got off the paddle wheeler. He would take his time, and after this journey by night, would travel only by day. Uzziah figured it would take him eight days to get close to Columbus, then close to the same amount of time to get to the Shenandoah Valley. He had a good horse, a life-saving donkey, and plenty of grub. He wasn't worried.

His camping he kept off the road and back into the woods, and seeing how the riff-raff that traveled up and down the road wanted whatever it was that you had, that they didn't. He kept to himself. Met some nice folks who wanted to travel with him, but he always told them he was going off to the east in a few miles, and when the first crossroads came up, he took it, confirming his explanation for not traveling with them, then he would get back on the main road north later.

He was about a good seven or so days out when he began to see the early morning smoke coming from a larger town when he rode up on the Scioto River. There was no bridge, so he rode Shadow into the river and swam for the other side. Jenny wasn't a good swimmer, but made it with as much braying as she could afford. She and Shadow shook off like dogs, then they made for the center of town. There were several saloons, maybe six in all, and he stopped at the one that looked the oldest. He tied Shadow up, walked to the batwing doors, and stood and looked over the clientele this time of day. It was the usual drunks, a card shark or two, and two saloon girls who looked like they'd seen better days.

He walked to the bar, and the barkeep walked right over, they weren't busy.

"Whiskey," he said, then changed his mind. "Is the beer cool?"

"Yeah, beer's good and cool."

"Just a draft," he said, got the beer, and turned around and looked at everyone who was looking at him, since he'd just gotten into town. They looked away immediately.

"Anybody here know a Loretta Stevens?" Uzziah

said loud enough for everybody to hear. Most did not look up.

He turned back to the barkeep. "How 'bout you?"

"Sheriff Martin's office is across the street, down two blocks," the barkeep offered.

Uzziah finished the beer and went back outside. Shadow was still a bit wet, and so was the saddle. A wind blew from the north down the main street, and Uzziah held onto his old slouch hat. He didn't much feel like running after it.

The day was coolish, probably in the '50s, but the sun was managing to shine through scattered clouds. He rode Shadow down the three blocks with Jenny hurrying after them, and there, on the other side of the street, was a sign, *Sheriff's Office*.

He rode up in front and the door was closed, but there was a window in the door, and he could see a man with a star on his chest looking through the window at him. He always carried his Hawken, and he had it in his right hand when he entered the office.

"Mornin'," Uzziah said, and remained standing.

"Any particular reason yer carrin' that cannon?" Sheriff Martin asked.

"It's sorta part of my body," Uzziah said.

Sheriff Martin stood and looked Uzziah up and down—deerskin clothes, long hair, long beard, and hard-working boots on his feet.

"What's a mountain man doin' this far east?" he said, sitting back down and indicating the chair across from his desk for Uzziah.

"Well, that's why I'm here, a...friend of mine asked me to look up his ma."

"What would that there friend's name be?"

"Benjamin Stevens."

"Uh-huh," the sheriff said, and was caught up in thought.

Uzziah just sat there. He'd learned a long time ago, lawmen were different than most. They held suspicions and carried a wealth of information about those they sheriffed.

"What ya wanna see her fer?" he asked and spat toward the spittoon, but missed. By the look of the wall and floor around the spittoon, that was his custom. Uzziah looked back at the sheriff.

"I'm only a terrible shot spittin', ifn ya pulled up that Hawken ya be dead afore it went off," Sheriff Martin said, and quite frankly, Uzziah believed the man. There was no correlation between spitting and shooting, at least not that Uzziah was aware of.

"Don't hafta worry 'bout that," Uzziah said, and he could tell, Sheriff Martin was still ready to draw in the next second. Martin didn't say anything, so Uzziah asked again, "Do ya know the woman, Loretta Stevens?"

"I do," was all the sheriff said.

"Can ya tell me where I might find the lady?"

"I could."

Uzziah sat there a bit, long enough for Sheriff Martin to gather his wits and tell him.

"Will ya?" Uzziah finally asked.

"I will."

Again, Uzziah sat there patiently waiting.

"We'll go together," Martin finally said, and he got up so quickly his chair hit the wall behind him, and he left it that way.

They walked out to the street, and Uzziah mounted

up, while the sheriff walked down a couple stores and retrieved his horse from a group that was tied there. He mounted up and they went back the way Uzziah had come into town.

"Knew a sheriff once, he'd tied his hoss outside his office, and the bank robbers shot it dead afore they robbed the bank. Always keep that in mind," Sheriff Martin said, and Uzziah wondered how many habits he had that were based on one bad experience.

They rode toward the Scioto River, and Uzziah couldn't help but wonder if he was going to have to swim the river on horseback again, but they turned down a dirt road that ran along the river on the dry side. Sheriff Martin wasn't a big man, and for lawmen, that was a plus in gunfights. Smaller targets were harder to hit. He had a handsome mustache and wore his hair short, but not clipped to the roots. Uzziah was impressed by his seat in the saddle and figured the man had at one time been a long rider.

"When ya stop herdin' cows?" Uzziah asked him while they were both in a comfortable lope.

"Who said I herded cows?" the sheriff asked.

"Ride like ya did."

Martin spat away from Uzziah, and he was glad for that. The left side of the sheriff's horse was splattered with tobacco spittle.

"Was a trail boss afore I took this job."

"Why'd ya quit?"

"Got tired of eating dust."

"Thought trail bosses rode off to the side with the chuck."

"Not ifn ya want those doing drag to do their jobs," he said, and indicated the farmhouse up alongside the river. It was built on stilts and quite large with a wraparound porch, which was probably good to sit on when the sun was going down, Uzziah thought.

Sheriff Martin saw Uzziah spying the house, and spoke up. "Loretta and her husband, he's dead now, but they put it up like that 'cause the Scioto floods in spring. Ifn ya look behind the stairs, y'all see a rowboat."

Uzziah looked, and surely enough, behind both staircases, there was a rowboat, which was landlocked now, but he was sure they came in handy when the river flooded. The barn was built on a knoll, which was west of the farm. Uzziah supposed that the Scioto never got that high.

"Hello, the house!" the sheriff yelled, and a fairly good-looking woman in her mid to late forties came out the front door with an apron on and a towel in her hand.

"Darlin'," she said, "whatcha doin' out chere this time a mornin'?"

"On business, actually," Sheriff Martin said, and he was all business. Uzziah figured he didn't like her calling him darling, but at least now he knew the reluctance of telling him where she lived.

They tied their horses to a hitching post and walked up the stairs, the sheriff taking the lead.

"This chere is—well, stranger, I ne'r got yer name."

"Uzziah O'Bannon," Uzziah said, and he waited to see if she would extend her hand, and when she did, he shook it once and let it go. He wasn't going to be kissing strange women's hands like Immanuel, especially since Sheriff Martin had already staked a claim, as it were.

"Pleased to meet ya, I'm—"

"Already knows yer name, I ask fer it, 'member?" the sheriff said.

"Would you like some coffee?" she asked both men.

"I would," Uzziah said, and he guessed she already knew the sheriff would.

They sat on the back porch overlooking the river, and the coffee was good, as good as Uzziah made, and that was saying something. He was about halfway through his cup when she spoke up.

"Charlie said ya asked fer me by name."

"Yes, ma'am, I got news concerning Benjamin—"

"I hope he ain't movin' back chere," the sheriff said.

"Charlie, stop it this minute," she scolded him.

"Sorry," was all the sheriff said, but now Uzziah knew Benjamin had been a problem here as well as in the mountains. Well, he was an excellent shot.

"What has my Benny done now?" she asked and followed in rapid succession, another question, "Ya don't look like no lawman."

"I'm not. Benjamin was a friend of mine," Uzziah said.

"I noticed ya used the word, *was*, what'd he do to bring ya back here to find him?"

"No, he don't need no findin', he's dead, ma'am," Uzziah said and looked her right in the face. She was hit by the news, but was late in reacting. When she did, it was like an expression of relief went over her face.

"How'd he die?"

"Bravely," Uzziah said, then added, "In my arms."

Which was a statement that was as true as true could be.

"Gunshot?"

"He was shot, all right," Uzziah agreed, since he had been the one to shoot off his right hand.

"Did ya bury him up thares in the mountains?"

"Yes, ma'am, we did."

"We?"

"He had a partner," Uzziah said, and wasn't going into the fact that he'd died on the same day, shot to death. "And some other friends, we took care of the whole thing," Uzziah said, remembering that he hadn't said anything over the graves which they dug up in the meadow.

"Who shot him?" she asked, and it was a legit question.

"He never saw the man that shot him," Uzziah said, telling the truth, since they had been sniping up above them when he shot Benjamin's hand off.

"Did ya catch the bastard?"

"Loretta!" the sheriff said, and Uzziah guessed he didn't like that sort of language from the woman he loved.

"Well," she said, looking right at Sheriff Martin, "did ya?"

"No, we didn't, sorry," Uzziah said, looking down at the river, which was flowing so peaceful.

"Just as well, I suppose," she said, then added, "His brothers and sisters are all working the farm now, can ya stay and have supper with us?"

Uzziah looked at the sheriff, and he could see that wasn't something Sheriff Charlie Martin wanted, and to tell the truth, neither did Uzziah.

"No, ma'am, I got many a mile afore I can rest, it's too early in the day fer me to stop."

"Well, daylight's burnin'," Sheriff Martin said as he stood up.

"One last question, did he say anythin' afore he died?"

"Yes, Loretta, he did, he asked me to come tell ya he was dead," Uzziah said.

"Well, good to know that he had such a good friend, who would travel all this way just to let a mother know," she said, and she grabbed Uzziah and held him and wept. It started out weak, but turned into a breakdown almost. Her shuddering reminded Uzziah of the way Benjamin had shuddered in his arms when his neck broke. It was an unholy memory, and now his ma was shuddering in the same way. He had a cool feeling go up his back like someone had stepped on his grave.

The two of them, Sheriff Martin and Uzziah, rode out to the road that passed by the Stevens' farm. Uzziah pulled his horse up and Sheriff Martin did, too.

"Ifn I go away from town, where will that take me?" Uzziah asked.

"West acourse," the sheriff said.

"That's good, that's the direction I wanna go."

"Son," Sheriff Martin said, now being nicer, since he knew why Uzziah wanted to see his Loretta.

"Yeah?"

"Ifn yer gonna travel along the Mississippi, avoid Nauvoo, Illinois."

"Why's that?"

"Oh yeah, ya been up in the Rockies away from all the falderal."

"What falderal would that be?" Uzziah asked,

thinking he'd been through his own version of some falderal back in St. Louis and Chicago.

"Them Mormons!" Sheriff Martin spat the words out like he was getting rid of a bad taste in his mouth.

"Who are the Mormons?"

"Just don't go there, the governor of Missouri, Lilburn Boggs, issued an execution order on them in 1838!"

"What kinda group are they that that would happen to 'em?"

"They's some weird group that follers Joseph Smith around like he's a god. Stay away from Nauvoo, son, just do it!" Sheriff Martin said, and turned his horse and literally galloped away from where Uzziah was sitting Shadow.

2

They had taken Immanuel James Jones down to his suite room on the paddle wheeler, and when they got a key from the bursar—Immanuel had given his to the Creole woman—they found that the entire cabin had been ransacked. Whoever had done it had taken everything—as in everything. His Hawken wasn't there, his mountain man deer skins were gone, even the good clothes that Uzziah had stacked in a neat pile were gone.

The only thing they left Immanuel were the clothes on his back, whatever money he had in his pockets, and Trevor, his horse. Well, they didn't know about the horse.

The doctor, a man by the name of Gâteaux, Dr. Steven Gâteaux, was from an old family in New Orleans, and he'd been on business for the family and was returning home. His family home was on the north side of the Mississippi.

When the paddle wheeler had finally docked and

Immanuel was out of the woods, so to speak, it was nearly four days since Uzziah had left the ship.

Charity Hospital had been erected in 1736 by a grant from Jean Louis, a French sailor and shipbuilder who had died the year before its construction. It was stated in his will that a hospital for those who lived in New Orleans was to be erected using his money. It was constructed at the intersection of Chartres Street and Bienville Street, where the Mississippi bends at Algiers Point.

The dock for the paddle wheeler was not far from neither Charity Hospital nor the Chartres Street House where Dr. Gâteaux lived.

The doctor had gotten off the ship with strict admonitions that Immanuel was not to be taken from his bedside till he returned. The doctor had figured out Immanuel's proclivities and stationed a very beautiful woman by him to ensure his instructions were followed.

Dr. Gâteaux found a wheeled chair which he bought and took onto the ship, and wheeled into Immanuel's suite, but both Immanuel and the beautiful young lady were not there. He ran outside the suite and found Immanuel about to walk down the gangplank with her.

"Stop! Stop!" he yelled, and they both turned to see who he was yelling at. "That man must not take another step, or you will be responsible for his death!" Dr. Gâteaux shouted as he ran toward the gangplank.

Immanuel turned to the young lady who could easily have been his granddaughter. "Is he yelling at us?"

"Monsieur, c'est vrai," she said, and Immanuel had no idea what that meant.

Dr. Gâteaux ran up, pushing the wheeled chair, and taking Immanuel by the arm, placed him unceremoniously into it.

"What's the meaning of this!?!" Immanuel asked.

"You may not walk as yet, I told you. You could have another angina pectoris, and that one may be your last," the good doctor said.

"Well, good, havin' the last of somethin' that's painful would be a blessin'."

"It would also be the end of your life, sir," Dr. Gâteaux said.

"Oh, yeah, that," Immanuel said, still unwilling to let go of the young lady's hand.

"As I explained to you, I will take you to the Charity Hospital, run by the Sisters of Charity, and there you will be able to make a full recovery."

"Can she come?" Immanuel asked.

"She's my granddaughter, and no, she will go home."

"Where's that?"

"At my Chartres Street House, where she will be staying with me for the next year," the doctor explained.

"You sure she can't come?" Immanuel asked, still not letting go of her hand.

She let out a stream of French about as fast as Immanuel had ever heard anyone speak any language, and the good doctor listened, then bowed his head.

"Yes, yes, she says she will accompany us to Charity Hospital," he said.

"Good for me," Immanuel said and smiled.

His color wasn't good, and his hand trembled ever so slightly. This was not the Immanuel who had boarded the paddle wheeler, and his recovery was just beginning. And yet, he would not let go of the fact that he was a lady's man, and would remain one till the day he died.

"Do they have whiskey at the hospital?" Immanuel asked.

"Certainly, but for medicinal purposes only," Dr. Gâteaux said.

"Oh, it's my kinda medicine, that's a fer sure," the mountain man said, all the while smiling at the doctor's granddaughter who walked alongside them as Dr. Gâteaux pushed the wheeled chair down the street.

3

There was something that Immanuel and Uzziah had in common. In fact, it was probably universal across most men. They didn't like to be told what to do, they just didn't! And Sheriff Martin's admonition about the Mormons was about as grating as it could be, and in reality, all it did was point Uzziah Ferguson O'Bannon right toward the town of Nauvoo, Illinois. It took him several days to wind his way in that direction, and whenever he went through some small town, he would stop someone on the street, or beside their pasture fence, and ask them a simple question, "Which way to Nauvoo?"

Most people looked at him as if he'd taken the Lord's name in vain, or cursed their dear old mother. And it was such a simple question. Sometimes, he got resistance: "Son, ya don't wanna go there." Or "Nauvoo, ya might as well be askin' the way to hell," one man had shouted, but pointed anyway.

Finally, when Uzziah had made a rise in the road, he saw at the top of the next hill the foundation of the most magnificent building he had ever seen in construction. That construction had been halted, and Uzziah wasn't sure why. He rode up and ground-tied Shadow, then walked within the foundational work that had been completed. He sat down on one of the stones which had not been raised up as yet, and pondered what this could be, and also wondered if this was Nauvoo.

He heard a pistol cock and turned to see another mountain man. His beard and hair were long, but his hairline was high, giving his forehead a most prominent seeing. He had a houndstooth scarf around his neck, and it hung between the vest and the coat he was wearing. He had on a hat much like Uzziah's and the most piercing blue eyes Uzziah had ever seen. His horse was ground-tied like Shadow on the other side of the foundation and his boots were muddy.

"What ta doin' here?" he asked, the gun never leaving Uzziah's midsection.

"I'm admiring this architecture," Uzziah said, then added, "I've never seen anything like it."

"And ya never will," the man said, never taking his eyes off Uzziah or his Hawken.

"I mean ya no harm," Uzziah said, looking directly into the man's blue eyes, and realized he was echoing the words of the dying man alongside the Mississippi River.

"Then, put the Hawken down there where yer seated, and stand up."

Uzziah did as he was ordered.

The man looked over at Shadow and smiled. "Nice horse, it'll be mine, ifn I hafta kill ya."

"That won't be necessary," Uzziah said.

"And why's that?"

"I'm Uzziah O'Bannon. Me and my partner were just tried for the murder of a Pinkerton Agent in Chicago," Uzziah said, wondering why the hell he was telling the man with the gun trained on him that he'd been tried for murder.

"I read somethin' 'bout that, ole hickory hisself stood up fer ya, didn't he?"

"Yeah, yeah, he did."

"We ain't had such luck with government officials, why the last state we was in Missouri, Governor Boggs put an extermination order out on us like we was some kinda vermin," he said and uncocked the pistol, put it back in his holster, and walked forward, stopping a short distance from Uzziah.

"Uzziah O'Bannon, it's a pleasure to meet ya, I'm Porter Rockwell, and this chere is gonna be the Nauvoo Temple of the Latter-Day Saints, more commonly called Mormons, though we ain't supposed to cotton to that name. Hey, just on the chance of it, ya got a bottle of whiskey on ya?" Porter asked, and his smile was infectious.

"I do, I do, in my saddlebags," Uzziah said.

Porter took him by the arm in a peaceful, gentle gesture and said, "Let's go see what kind."

They walked together, and Uzziah noticed that the right leg of Porter's was shorter than the left and he walked with a noted limp.

Porter saw Uzziah looking down at his leg.

"Yeah, it's a fer sure limp, all right. The Prophet Joseph Smith's got one, too, but fer different reasons. His is from typhoid fever, which affected the growth of his leg, mine's from a poorly set ankle bone. But we grew up neighbors, he's eight years older, and when I was but sixteen, I was the first one baptized into his church."

Uzziah opened the saddlebag and Porter brought the pistol back up on him, just in case there was something besides a bottle of whiskey in there. Uzziah pulled out a bottle of Jameson whiskey, and the look on his new friend, Porter Rockwell's, face was something to behold. Porter suggested they go back to his campfire, which was close to the work being done on the foundation.

Uzziah took up Shadow's reins and followed Porter, whose limp was no better when he wasn't holding someone's arm.

"Damn, how many people ya hafta kill to get that there hoss?"

"Shadow's been mine fer a while, won't let no one else ride 'im, so it's not like he could be stolen."

"Interestin', yes sir, that certainly is!"

Porter's horse was a nice-looking roan mare, and Shadow took interest right away.

"Now ifn yer stud wants to mount my Ludean, well, he's more than welcomed," Porter said and chuckled. Uzziah looked at him funny, and Porter walked over and took Ludean's saddle and bridle off. "There, she's a waitin'," he said.

Uzziah got up and took off Shadow's saddle and bridle, and the two horses ran off, but not too far.

"See, what I tell ya, Ludean ain't ever met a stud that don't like her."

"Where is everybody?" Uzziah asked, pointing around the site where the building of the temple was going on.

"They ain't workin' acause it's a Sunday. Lord took Sunday off, and so do we saints," Porter Rockwell said, licking his lips as he looked at the bottle whose seal had not been broken.

"You do the honors," Uzziah said, sensing that he was dealing with a thirst which he had known before. He handed the bottle across the fire to where Porter was sitting.

"Well, you are a scholar and gentleman, ain't ya?"

He reverently took the seal off and twisted the cork out so that it would not break. He held the newly opened bottle under his nose and breathed in.

"Ah, now that's a lovely smell," he said, then raised the bottle to Uzziah and took a very healthy pull. Then, wiping his mustache with the back of his sleeve, he handed the bottle back to Uzziah. Uzziah raised the bottle high as if he were drinking just as much, but he had learned with Immanuel that it was always best if there was one person among those drinking who had their wits about them.

They kept drinking like that for the better part of half an hour, when Porter Rockwell spoke up. His voice sounded exactly the same, you couldn't tell he'd had anything to drink, but the story he told was one loosened by whiskey.

"Ya know, Governor Boggs was a practical man. He'd seen what we'd done around Kirkland, and the progress we'd made, and he had so many complaints about us. They saw multiple women living with the same man, whether in one house or different homes. That sent them into a frenzy, and when those who are different from ya have more than what others considered their share, well, there goes the commandment about not coveting what yer brother has," Porter said and took another swig. "Awful nice of ya to share like this, brother Uzziah."

"How many wives do ya have?" Uzziah asked.

"Well, that's fer me to know, and fer ya to find out, ain't it? Only kidding, she's Luana Hart Rockwell, and she's bore me three children. Emily, who's seven years old, Caroline, who's five years old, and my son, Orin Porter Rockwell Jr. He just turned two, he did," Porter said, and then he laughed. Uzziah hadn't heard anyone laugh like that except Immanuel. It came from the belly, and it was all heart. He looked ridiculous laughing and didn't seem to mind. It was positively infectious. Both men laughed together there for the first time, and the loneliness that Uzziah had felt leaving Immanuel evaporated. It surprised him, and immediately he expected it to come back, but whenever he was in the presence of Porter Rockwell, it never did.

Porter looked at the bottle, it was nearly three-quarters empty, and said, "Ya know, let's go into Nauvoo and see my family afore I get too far into this bottle. I want them to meet ya." As the two men were getting up, they looked, and Shadow had just dismounted from Ludean, and they were running around together. Him following her as was their custom.

"Let's round up the naughty children, shall we?" Porter said.

They rode into Nauvoo and Uzziah was struck by not only the fine construction of the houses and the community buildings in the downtown area, but also the manner in which they were kept up. The place looked as crisp as the first day it had come together. *As if God himself were staying there, and they were making it look nice for him*, Uzziah thought.

They rode to the middle of town, where wagons abounded, and as they passed one freight wagon in particular, Uzziah saw two small children sitting in the back of the wagon, and seated upon the buckboard as he passed, a young lady of maybe eighteen years of age, turned her bonneted head and looked right into Uzziah's blue eyes.

Uzziah was dumbstruck and pulled up his horse, Shadow, stopping to stare at her.

Porter was not that far behind, but he was feeling his oats, having drunk most of the bottle of Jameson by himself, and for no particular reason, he pulled out his Navy Colt and fired it into the air.

The young lady who had hold of the reins of the two horses looked scared as the horses reared up, then took off down the street. The father of the young girl, it must have been him, because he came from the mercantile store opposite the wagon and dropped what he was carrying as he ran down the boardwalk to no avail after the wagon.

The small boy and girl in the back of the runaway wagon were screaming as Porter rode fast past Uzziah on Ludean. It didn't take Uzziah to realize that if anyone was going to catch that runaway freight wagon, it wasn't going to be the roan mare, it was going to be Shadow.

By the time Uzziah passed Porter on Ludean, they were outside the town and heading into a wooded area. Much to the young lady's credit, she was still holding onto the reins and pulling back as hard as she could. But the faces of the horses, even with the reins pulled back like that, were resolute. They weren't going to stop no matter what!

As Uzziah made the side of the wagon, the brim on his slouch hat was pinned back against his forehead, and he was leaning into Shadow's gallop. The girl momentarily looked over to see who it was who had ridden out after her, and when she saw it was the man she had seen in town just before the runaway team got started, she smiled.

Uzziah smiled back and, leaning forward, spoke into Shadow's ear.

"Let's pass 'em, boy!" he whispered, and Shadow found the extra depth to his run, and fairly soon, Uzziah was alongside the runaway team. He thought about reaching down and grabbing the leads to the two horses, but decided that at his weight, he just might fall off, then all would be lost. Looking ahead, he saw that there was a fast-moving stream up ahead. That meant that the horses would hit the stream at full tilt, and who knew what could happen then?

He jumped from Shadow's back, and no one was more surprised than himself, and of course, Shadow. He landed between the two runaway horses, and for a moment, his boots scratched along the rough road, but he pulled them up, and taking both bridles in his hands, he pulled back with what, later, Porter Rockwell would swear was strength from above.

The horses balked at first, but the pressure was too much as they slowed and eventually came to a stop at the edge of the stream.

Porter rode up and, hollering, almost got the

horses started again. Uzziah gave him a dirty look, and the mountain man of Nauvoo whispered, "Brother, I ain't ever seen anything like that. Wait till I tell the prophet what ya done. That gal there is his second cousin's daughter, and ifn anything had happened to her, ough wee! There would have been hell to pay!"

"I do not like being talked about as if I were not here, and the mentioning of perdition does nothing but bring it our way," the young lady chastised Porter, still sitting all proper up there on the buckboard.

"Sorry, Hannah, no disrespect meant," Porter said. "I'd like ya to meet the man who done saved yer bacon. This chere is Uzziah O'Bannon."

Uzziah had gotten off the team of wagon horses, none too graciously, and he walked back to where Hannah was extending her hand. He took her hand and raised it to his lips, and she allowed it, which surprised Porter, and then Uzziah kissed Hannah Larue's hand, and truthfully, she did not mind it.

The two children who had been in the back were less reserved. They knew what happened when wagons wrecked. They came up and both of them, still crying, wrapped their arms around Uzziah's neck. He loved children and hugged them back. Uzziah climbed up into the wagon to drive it back into town.

"It's okay, you're okay now, you're safe," he whispered to them, and he did not see it, but Hannah was enthralled by this behavior. So many men were gallant enough, but not enough of them knew the hearts of children, and this man certainly did. He calmed them down in no time at all, and they moved up between Hannah and Uzziah. The little girl sat right next to

Uzziah. The boy wanted to sit there, but he let her, after all, she was his younger sister.

Porter stood there watching the two of them, the big mountain man from the Rockies and the petite and lovely Hannah Larue, and he marveled. No one could predict what God, the Father, had in store for any of us, and here was a prime example. Now, he was a Gentile, and she the second cousin to the Prophet Joseph Smith, but if this was meant to be, as much as Porter imagined in his addled brain that it was, then God would find a way.

Uzziah saw Shadow grazing on some grass nearby. "Porter, do ya mind, grab up Shadow and tie him to the back of the wagon."

Porter walked over, picked up the reins, and Shadow looked at him strangely. He tied the reins to the back of the freight wagon and Porter mounted back up and rode alongside the lovely couple. Porter looked at her, but she looked at him once, then averted her gaze, and he knew why. She had let a stranger kiss her hand, and when she looked at Porter, he could tell she didn't want that kiss, even on the hand, reported in Nauvoo. It wouldn't be, Porter knew how to keep his own counsel.

When they rode back into town, there was a crowd of sorts, people who had been shopping, or going about their own business, and they had lined the boardwalks to see what would happen. They applauded, waved their hats, and cheered. Uzziah was quite amazed! It was as if they were greeting a long-lost friend.

Then, he saw a man who had no beard. His hair was golden in the sunlight, and he was dressed quite well in a blue frock coat, yellow suede vest, and a white tie about his neck. He was looking at Hannah. Uzziah figured it was to see if she was okay, but when his gaze turned to Uzziah, it stayed there for a bit, then he smiled.

Uzziah had been smiled at by the 7th President of these United States, and by others who held position in this life, but there was something about that particular man's smile which was enchanting.

Uzziah pulled the wagon up right where it had been before the horses bolted away with it, near an older man, presumably Hannah's father.

The two little ones started going on about what had happened.

"Father, you should have seen him! This man is an angel sent from God," the little girl said.

The boy joined in. "Plus he gots a faster horse than anybody in Nauvoo!" and everyone laughed at that, even Porter.

Ephrem Larue stuck out his hand, and Uzziah took it.

"You may indeed be a Godsend, that remains to be seen, but if you hadn't saved these children and my oldest daughter, my wife, Glade, would surely have had my hide!" he said, and there was an agreement and laughter from some of those crowded around.

The man Uzziah had seen with the golden hair and the fine clothing, walked up, actually, he had a slight limp like Porter had said, and Uzziah knew who he was.

"Sir," he said with a strong and orotund voice. "This day, I have seen you in our midst, and it is not everyone who comes here and immediately saves. Therefore, you are, without doubt, a protector and deliverer of this town, much like our own Porter Rockwell, and I can see that you have already met and affirmed your friendship. What did your mother call you?"

"Uzziah Ferguson O'Bannon."

"Uzziah Ferguson O'Bannon, step down and be welcomed into our Latter-Day Saint's community of Nauvoo!"

Uzziah got down and was surprised when he was embraced by the prophet. The people around made a noise of both surprise and wonder. Evidently, Joseph Smith did not embrace total strangers, but then again, Uzziah had saved his first cousin, Hannah Larue.

"Tonight, will you please join me and my family at our home. There will be a feast in your honor, and Ephrem, you and your family must also come," the prophet said.

The next few moments were lost on Uzziah as those gathered around all came forward and shook his hand, and welcomed him to Nauvoo. It would have been one thing if those who did this had done it because they felt they must, but Uzziah was a good judge of character, and these people were honestly welcoming him. Perhaps they had had so much of the discrimination of those who hated them and their kind, that just having someone who had, without thought, rescued one of their own, perhaps that was enough, but about a half hour later, when Porter walked up and the greetings had stopped, Uzziah felt something, and he wasn't sure what it was.

"They got ya, didn't they?" Porter asked.

"Whatcha mean?"

"The way they truly welcomed ya, I mean, we couldn't have rehearsed a better welcome for ya, could we?" and Porter winked.

Oh my God, thought Uzziah, *Porter had risked the lives of those children and that beautiful young lady by firing off his Navy Colt*! Had that been what happened? Well, he had winked when he'd said what he'd said. But how, why? Uzziah was a bit confused when Porter took him by the arm.

"Where we goin'?" Uzziah asked the man who might have engineered his welcome in Nauvoo. He wanted to ask Porter, but then he didn't. It was so confusing.

"We are gonna go to the bar where I tend the boards," Porter said, and they walked down the street, crossed over, then went toward a pond, where there was a place which looked like no saloon that Uzziah had ever seen.

The place was surrounded by windows, and open in the front and in the back. There was a fine bar that served spirits and a back porch where those who wanted to drink and watch the ducks and geese swim the pond could do so.

"Bar's open!" Porter yelled, and those who were sitting around got up and wandered, no hurry in their step at all, to the bar, where Porter had put on his clean white apron and started serving them. Uzziah's only thought was, *This must be what a saloon in heaven would look like!*

Then, Uzziah's heart was pierced by the loneliness that can only come when a dear friend or relative had passed. He sat down there at one of the back tables and knew that this place would be a place that Immanuel, himself, would celebrate. He certainly would like all the pretty young women who were in Nauvoo. He sat there and began to mourn his friend. He wondered what, if anything, had happened to Immanuel. He knew in his bones that something had, and he was about to get depressed when a hand was laid upon his shoulder. He looked up and Porter was standing there with a cool beer in his hand.

Uzziah took the beer and Porter had another one in the other hand for himself, and he sat. They looked at each other as men do over a mug of suds, and thoughts of a perished Immanuel just lost themselves into the thin air.

4

Immanuel James Jones was well known around Charity Hospital. It didn't matter, it seemed, how old the nurses were, or whether they were called nuns or not. When the man got a chance, he pinched their bottoms.

He'd been there for nearly a month, and he was getting better, because sometimes, when he pinched the bottoms of the younger nuns, he had it in his mind that they should do more than simply screech at him and give him an ugly look. He was thinking about sneaking out of the hospital and going to what the locals called the Quarter, where, evidently, a man could get whatever he wanted. He missed his whiskey, that was true, but mostly he missed the brotherhood of other men who wanted to enjoy life. And secretly, he missed one Uzziah Ferguson O'Bannon, and he wasn't quite sure why. Yeah, they had been partners for nearly ten years, that was true enough, and they had variously saved each other's bacon from time to time, but it wasn't that.

Every time he tried to argue with the doctors or

nurses, they wouldn't argue back! What was wrong with these people!?! He wanted to get into a heated argument with someone who could hold his own and give tit for tat, but there was only one he'd ever met who could do that, and that man had left his fancy clothes and ridden back to the life that they both loved.

What was he, Immanuel James Jones, doing in this huge city, a city which had had such a hospital for hundreds of years, when the rest of the county it was now in barely had hospitals at all? Where were those of equality? Where was a man who could hold his own, both in liquor and dialogue?

He found himself truly a stranger in a strange land, and he had to get out of there—well, out of the hospital! He was having all these thoughts when Dr. Gâteaux entered his room, which was part of a greater ward of sick men, but had been cordoned off by panels of white, which were flowing in the wind at this moment.

"Doctor, I am so glad yer chere!"

Dr. Gâteaux looked at Immanuel as if he were looking at a spoiled child.

"Sir, I'm afraid the staff at Charity Hospital had grown weary of you!"

"And I, them!"

"Well, then, I have come up with the perfect answer to this," Gâteaux said.

"Tell me 'bout it."

"You are going to stay at my Chartres Street House."

"Really, yer gonna let me into yer house?"

"Yes, but there will be rules, Immanuel, and the first time you step out of the boundaries of those rules, you will be put out of my house. Do you understand?" Dr. Gâteaux asked.

"Yes, yes, of course, there are always rules," Immanuel said, but what he was thinking about was the granddaughter of the doctor, the beautiful young lady who had been so kind to him on board the ship and had helped him to the gangplank. Of course, he wanted the young woman, even if it meant going behind the good doctor's back, and he knew, Immanuel knew, in his heart of hearts, if he was to do that, he would be a most despicable person, but to be able to put himself inside that beautiful body, well, it might just be worth it.

The doctor's beautiful home was in a Quarter of New Orleans, which was essentially influenced by the French. The land was originally owned by the Ursuline nuns, who sold off portions of their land in 1825. The design was by Francois Correjolles and built by the constructed by the builder James Lambert in 1826, so it was basically a newer home in the area. Within the house were elements of a Creole cottage with Grecian revival features, including a Palladian façade. Most of the interior rooms were copying the Creole style, as was the elevated section in the rear of the house, where the consul of Switzerland's wife, when they had owned the house, had added the adjoining gardens.

The house from the outside was deceptively ordinary, but once inside the front foyer, the long hallway had features like a grandfather's clock and French doors leading into rooms, which led eventually to the parlor with the piano forte, and spectacular views of the courtyard, which extended to the gardens beyond. When leaving to go out on the porch, which surrounded the whole of the back of the house, one realized that they were on the second floor of the house. The Chartres Street entrance actually entered on the second level of the house.

Immanuel was exhausted by the time they got there. The walk from his hospital room to the front of Charity Hospital, then the wheelchair ride to the carriage, which Dr. Gâteaux provided. The carriage ride there was pleasant, and the day was warm despite the fact that it was well into November.

Once there, Immanuel had steps to ascend to get to the main entrance. He was enchanted by the long hallway leading to the back of the house, and expected at any moment to see the beautiful granddaughter of the doctor. When they were standing on the porch surrounding the back, Immanuel finally spoke up. "Where's your granddaughter?"

The doctor looked at him for a while before he spoke. "Her room is an undisclosed portion of this home, and at present she is away at boarding school in Baton Rouge."

"But I thought you said she lived here?"

"She does when she isn't in school. Christmas will be here soon, and she will be here for almost a month," the doctor said, pleased that the lure of his granddaughter had gotten the wastrel to come to a place where he would no longer be a public embarrassment to the Gâteaux family. Until Christmas, then, the doctor had nothing to worry about, or so he thought.

5

Able-bodied men in and near Nauvoo were asked to donate their labor to help extract stone from nearby quarries and haul it to the temple site. This was something that even Porter Rockwell helped with, and since his new best friend was Uzziah, he found himself deep in the quarry cutting out rock, helping them load it up, and transporting it to the building site. At the building site, men more proficient in the art of building, architecture, and planning, put their heads together, and through a pulley system, brought the chiseled rocks into place, and the building of the Nauvoo Temple progressed.

The night at the prophet's supper, Uzziah's first night in Nauvoo, they had talked about such work, but Uzziah's mind had been on other things.

As he watched the parents of all the children interact with them, he began to think that fatherhood would be good for him, very good. Hadn't he had a prime example of what it meant in his own father, Sean O'Bannon? No wonder Immanuel saw women as only toys for pleasure, his upbringing hadn't exactly instilled in him the idea that he, too, could be a father.

Across from him at the table were Porter, his wife, Luana, and seated beside Porter on the other side was his oldest daughter, Emily, whom Porter had mentioned was seven years old. She was her father's girl and doted on him constantly. When the large plates with the food were passed around, she served her father before she served herself, and as Uzziah looked around the table, he realized all the children had taken on expanded roles in their families, daughters serving fathers, brothers, and acting much more mature than their ages. It must have something to do with Joseph Smith. It had to. Before the meal had begun, the prophet stood, and everyone quieted down.

"Pray with me," the Prophet Joseph Smith said, "Heavenly Father, we are here this evening to bless this food, but even more than that, we are here because you have given us safe passage on our way to where we will establish and perfect your bride for your return. As we continue with the building of the temple, please help us remember that we are not building this temple for ourselves, but for the Second Coming of our Lord and Savior, Jesus Christ. Bless also all those at this table, especially our new friend, Uzziah O'Bannon, who thinks he accidentally found this place."

There was a little chuckling, then the prophet continued, "We know better. Each of us has wandered into your grace and each of us is better for it. And whom should he have found first, but Orin Porter Rockwell, the first to ever be baptized into this faith. Accidents, Lord, are for those Gentiles who have persecuted us. Accidents, Lord, are for those who look upon our happiness and can see nothing but their own tragedy. Deliver us as you delivered the Israelites of old, from bondage to the Promised Land, where we will welcome you in your second coming. We pray all of this in the name of our brother, Jesus, Amen."

Uzziah had wanted to sneak a look at Hannah Larue, and much to his surprise, she was looking directly at him. She shut her eyes quickly and pretended that she hadn't looked, but she had, and Uzziah was mightily glad. What did it mean? Why was she looking at him? Maybe it was because he had possibly saved her life, but just maybe, just maybe, she was as interested in him as he was in her.

During the meal, everyone looked to the prophet for his advice, if it were needed, but mostly the meal happened like meals happen every day. There was food, and laughter, and even a little wine was served by the prophet's barkeep, Porter Rockwell.

All these thoughts were going through Uzziah's mind as he was helping with the cutting of the stones used for the temple, and then someone screamed, "Look out!"

Uzziah instinctively moved away from the stone they were cutting, and it was a good thing, as it crashed down upon the wagon he was standing in, trying to guide it to rest there.

The wagon was smashed to bits, and Porter came over to Uzziah. "Brother, ya okay?"

"Yeah, I was thinkin' 'bout somethin' else," Uzziah said.

"Ya mean, someone else?" Porter teased.

Uzziah looked at the man who was quickly becoming his good friend and knew that he was right.

"Look," Porter began anew. "Ifn she's gonna cause yer death then ya might as well have a talk with her and ease yer mind, what say you?"

"But how?"

"I'll take ya over to Ephrem's house tonight after work, and while you two visits on the front porch, I'll pour Ephrem some of my good wine."

That night, Porter and Uzziah went back to Porter's home. It had a good tack room in the barn, and Uzziah and Porter had turned it into a good enough place for him to sleep. Porter had dragged out an old potbellied stove that kindly reminded Uzziah of the cabins in the mountains, and they fired it up that day, after putting in the chimney.

Uzziah went down to the stream and washed up, and when he came back, Porter had laid out some clothes on the bunk in the tack room. They were more or less traditional Mormon dress. The broadcloth was black, and the pants hung nicely from the suspenders and fit him, too. The muslin shirt, which he pulled over his head, tucked in nicely, and there was a string black tie that he tied in a small mirror that Luana had placed on top of the clothes. Uzziah had hung it on a nail in the tack room.

He looked at himself and looked prosperous and fine, but when he put on the flat, broad-brimmed black hat, he was turned into one of the prophet's soldiers. He liked the way he looked. When he came in to supper, everyone at Porter's table applauded, and Porter whistled loudly with only his lips. His daughters put their hands over their ears, and the two-year-old Orin Jr. started to cry.

"I've told you not to whistle in the house, and I won't tell you again," Luana said sternly as she turned to Uzziah. "You look like a saint."

"You're too kind," Uzziah replied, but the smile she gave him made him wonder how he would be received at the Larue home.

After supper, Porter kissed his wife and his three children, and the two men walked the short distance to the home of Ephrem Larue. They stood out on the oiled street, where the dust was never blown up, and both men looked through the curtained windows. They could see that the women were clearing the table, and the men were sitting back.

There she was, Hannah Larue. The grace with which she moved startled Uzziah, and he remembered how she had handled herself on the runaway buckboard and realized it was the same grace that had allowed her to be unruffled and calm when the entire event was over. He also thought about Porter firing off his weapon and was about to ask him if he had done it so that he, Uzziah, could ride to her rescue, but when he turned to ask and Porter had instinctively felt him looking at him and he, too, turned to hear what Uzziah was about to say, the front door of the Larue home was opened, and it was Ephrem.

"Well, kinda expected this, come on up," he said, and the two men standing in the street wandered right up on Ephrem's porch.

Uzziah wondered how this was going to be done when Porter spoke, "Uzziah's come to speak to Hannah."

Well, thought Uzziah, *that's how it was to be done.*

Porter then tilted the bottle toward Ephrem, and it was caught by the light from the parlor. Ephrem did nothing but pat Porter on the back, and they walked into the home. Porter put his hand out and said, "No, stay here, she's comin' out to ya."

Uzziah wondered about that, was it proper, and such things as that, when the screen creaked open and there she was standing with the door in her hand, and the light falling across her face. Her skin was like porcelain, her hand the smallest and most perfect hand Uzziah had ever seen, and when she spoke, the words literally melted his heart.

"Have you come to converse with me?" she asked, her eyes smiling like they were when she snuck that look at him at the prophet's supper table.

"Yes, I have," Uzziah almost whispered, and that made Hannah walk closer, which was not his intention, but he was glad he'd spoken so softly.

"I couldn't quite hear you, which is unusual for a man of your height and weight."

Momentarily, he wondered if she thought him fat, but dismissed the notion entirely.

"Yes, I've come to speak with ya," he finally got out.

She motioned behind him, and as he turned, she was by his side as she went to the porch swing, which was in full view of the parlor and everyone in it. In fact, they could hear the muffled conversation in the parlor as Uzziah supposed theirs could also be heard.

She was holding the swing and waiting for him to sit, as if she knew it would move the swing, his girth and all. He sat and she sat on the opposite side, putting her delicate arm, which was exposed from the elbow down, since she'd started with the dishes before she had been informed that there was a gentleman caller.

They sat there for a spell, and she was looking at him, but he was almost afraid to look at her, and he wondered why. All day long, he'd done nothing but think about her, and it had almost gotten him killed, and here they were sitting right together on the front porch of her pa's house, and he wouldn't look at her.

"Did you come here to stare at the porch flooring, Uzziah O'Bannon?" she asked sweetly.

He looked at her and she was smiling.

"Well, did you?"

"No ma'am," he said.

"That's what you would say to my ma, Uzziah, you may call me Hannah, since, in fact, that is my name."

"Hannah," he whispered without looking at her.

"Yes, Uzziah?" and he took a good look at this young—she couldn't be over nineteen years of age—woman, who was challenging him.

"Somethin' happens to me when I looks at you," he said.

"Is it the same something that happens to me?"

"I think so."

"I think so, too. Are you a Godly man, Uzziah O'Bannon?"

"Ifn ya mean do I read scripture and think 'bout doin' right, then the answer is yes," he said.

"That's good. You may be a Gentile, but you are known by Christ."

"He's my Savior."

"So, you've been baptized?"

"Back home in Virginia, yes."

"How old were ya?"

"Twelve."

"That's a good age, I have a brother that age."

"I gots ten brothers and sisters," Uzziah said, smiling.

"Are you sure you're not a Latter-Day Saint?" she said joking, since their families tended to be larger than most.

"Baptist."

She took something from her dress, it must have been in a pocket, and when she pulled it out, it seemed to him as if it might be a weapon, he was slightly startled and reached for his pistol when she said, "This is the Book of Mormon." Then she added, "If you want to court me, and I think you do, then read this, and talk to the Elders and Deacons about it, or better yet, talk to the prophet. He likes you, and some think he's too trusting, but he's an excellent judge of character."

Uzziah held the book like he would hold a Bible, because to Hannah, it was her Bible. He didn't know anything about the book, but was inspired by her words to read every bit of it.

"Will you read it?"

He just looked at her as she got up, leaned toward him, and kissed him on the cheek. He froze as if he were dreaming, and the next thing he heard was the screen door closing. Porter must have known it would be a short visit, for he was standing there.

"How'd it go?" Porter asked.

"She gave me this," Uzziah said, and held out the book.

"And she asked ya to read it, no doubt?"

"Yeah," he was thumbing through it, looking at the size of the print and the quantity of the pages.

"Well, ya like her, right?"

"Of course!"

"And it has to be read afore ya see her again, right?"

"How'd ya know that?"

"She's a good Latter-Day Saint woman, that's how's I know."

That night, when Uzziah went back to the tack room, he did not immediately go to sleep. Instead, he sat up on the bunk with his saddle behind him and started in on the Book of Mormon. When he put down the book, the light from the false dawn was coming through the slats in the tack room. He took out his chronometer and couldn't quite believe his eyes. It was time to work. He pulled up his suspenders and splashed water in his face on the way to the house.

Luana's breakfast was something that he found himself looking forward to. The biscuits, he had to ask her how she got them so fluffy, and the ham, well, he was sure that had something to do with the hogs that Porter raised, but they must have done something in the curing of the meat. He had smelled the woodsmoke coming from the smokehouse and thought that must be the trick in that smokehouse. He would ask Porter later about it.

They worked all day, and he was sure that he was going to be really tired before the day was over, then he remembered his scripture from his Bible he read that morning, like he always did.

He gives strength to the weary and increases the power of the weak. Even youths grow tired and weary, and young men stumble and fall, but those who hope in

the Lord will renew their strength. They will soar on wings like eagles, they will

run and not grow weary, they will walk and not faint
—Isaiah, 40:29-31

At one point, as they were hoisting a rather huge cut stone from the quarry, he looked over, and Porter was scratching his head, well, mentally, the rest of him was helping with the cut stone. They got it in the wagon, and as the wagon rode away, Porter spoke up.

"Brother, ya did not sleep last night. Ain't that what ya told me?"

"That's right."

"Ya read the Book of Mormon all night, and without sleep yer workin' like two men yer size."

"Whacha tryin' to say 'bout my size?" he asked half-joking.

Porter cracked up, and fairly soon, both of them were laughing, with the other men on the crew looking at them strangely.

"Ya wouldn't understand," Porter said to the rest of the crew.

Uzziah worked through the rest of the day, and the next and the next, and after nearly three days of reading at night and no sleep, he was fairly sure he'd seen angels and knew where the golden plates were hidden. When he got home on the fourth day, and his work had not dwindled in the least, he told Porter something.

"I won't be comin' to supper tonight, I'm gonna go

straight to bed. Tell Ephrem I will be at his house for dinner tomorrow night. Don't wake me till it's time to get ready for that supper, ya understand?"

Porter Rockwell smiled. "Ya gonna ask fer her hand, ain't ya?"

"I'm gonna do whatever it takes to make Hannah Larue my wife. Even if I have to walk through the depths of hell, I will have her as my wife!"

"All right, a little unorthodox, but I'll tell Ephrem just like ya asked."

When Uzziah was sleeping, he had a dream about his mama. She was smiling and praying for him. He knew Rahab wanted what was best for him, and he knew that Hannah was what was best. He tried to find his pa, and brothers and sisters to talk to them about his upcoming wedding, but he couldn't find them, then his mama said, "A man ought to marry a reasonable facsimile of his mother, otherwise he will never be happy."

He awoke from the dream, and it was the day after yesterday, and there was a knocking at the tack room door. When he answered it, it was Porter.

"Brother, time to go to the Larues' home," was all Porter said as he turned and went back to his home.

Uzziah went down to the river with a bar of lye soap and washed himself about as clean as he ever had been. He wanted his appearance above all else to please the Larues, especially Hannah.

As they walked the oiled road to the Larues' home, Uzziah was smiling.

"Yer pretty confident, ain't ya?"

"Acourse, God wants this," Uzziah said, still smiling.

"Yer that confident, well, good fer ya, young son," Porter said, and immediately Uzziah thought of Immanuel and wondered what he would think of this. Well, it really didn't matter, did it? He had a new life, and this life didn't include an old drunk and his tendencies. That was that!

Then, they were standing at the Larues' door. Porter knocked, and it was Hannah who opened the door. She smiled at Uzziah as if Porter wasn't there at all. "Come into our home, good Mormon men," she said.

The meal, well, Uzziah ate, but he'd be hard pressed to tell anyone what it was he ate, in fact, he was sure he had at least two helpings of everything, with Hannah's ma smiling like it was her hand that was going to be asked for.

As dessert, and he remembered what that was, one of his favorites, hot peach cobbler from the peaches that the Larues had grown, and homemade ice cream on top, which their younger children had churned.

"Ephrem, there's something I'd like to ask you, sir," Uzziah said, and no one was surprised at the table of ten people sitting there.

Hannah's sisters were holding their hands across their mouths, and her brothers simply laughed out loud, until their pa looked at them with the sternest look Uzziah had ever seen, then the man turned to Uzziah and smiled. "What's yer question, Uzziah?"

"I would like to have your daughter Hannah's hand in marriage?"

Hannah squealed like she'd just jumped from the

hayloft to the deep pile of soft hay below, and her sisters got up and ran to her chair, surrounding her with their love.

"You may ask me, and my answer will be *yes*, but you must also ask the Prophet Joseph Smith," Ephrem said.

Well, Uzziah was thrilled that Hannah's pa had said yes, and obviously so was she, but he hadn't counted on asking the prophet anything.

After supper, Uzziah and Hannah sat on the same porch swing that they had first talked on, and he held her hand, and she certainly didn't seem to object.

"Why do I gots to talk to Joe Smith?" Uzziah asked.

"No one calls the prophet that," she objected.

"Well, still, why?"

"I know ya read the entire book in three days, the talk of that feat has filled the gossiping of Nauvoo for all those days. A Gentile holding up in a tack room and reading night and day, and not eating. My goodness, Uzziah, you are truly a local hero," she said, smiling and moving closer to him on the swing. He could feel the heat of her thigh coming through and heating his leg, and, embarrassing as it was, he started to feel funny in his groin, and he knew what was happening. He sure hoped her mother didn't walk out, and he'd have to stand, she would know for sure what had happened to him.

"Whatcha talkin' 'bout, girl?"

"Ya saved me and my little brother and sister when the wagon took off," she began and he remembered he still hadn't asked Porter why he'd fired off his pistol like that. She added, "Then, after I gave you God's revelation to the prophet, you read it in three days, the same amount of time that it took Jesus to rise up from the dead," she said, glowing.

"Now, ya dun gone too far, Hannah. I want ya to be my wife, but ya can't be sayin' things that line me up with Jesus," he said, looking down at the planks on the porch again, because he was secretly thrilled that she had said what she had said.

"You did read it all, yes?" she asked, not quite believing it.

"Without a bit of sleep," he said, wanting to tell her about how he thought he'd seen where the golden tablets were buried, but thinking that was just a fever dream.

"What's your favorite passage, darling?" she asked him, and he was nearly bowled over by her calling him by such an endearing name.

"Well, don't you have one?" she asked again.

Uzziah just began with a memorized passage, truly his favorite, as she sat there amazed.

"*And he hath brought to pass the redemption of the world, where he that is found guiltless before him at the judgment day hath it given unto him to dwell in the presence of God in his kingdom, to sing ceaseless praises with the choirs above unto the Father, and unto the son, and unto the Holy Ghost, which are one God, in a state of happiness which hath no end.* Mormon 7:7"

When Uzziah had finished with the only scripture he had memorized, and he wasn't sure why he had done it, it simply appealed to him. Hannah grabbed him with her left hand around the back of the neck and brought his face to hers, where she bestowed upon him the first of many kisses to come.

Something happened to Uzziah when her lips met

his. He wasn't sure he was still on earth. He had spent so much time reading that book that in some ways he had been transported back to the time of the angel Maroni, and this kiss from the one whom he wanted above all else went straight to his head, as if he'd not eaten in days and been given the strongest whiskey that had ever been distilled.

As she pulled away, and it felt as if the kiss had lasted a day or two, he felt, truly felt, that if he were denied more of those same kisses that he just might die. They were as if the breath of life to him, truly.

When he finally opened his eyes, she had gone. He hadn't felt her get up, or hadn't heard the screen door either, but standing in front of him was Porter, smiling.

"Brother, ya's are truly smitten, ain't ya?"

Uzziah didn't say anything so that his lips would actually do something after they had been blessed with the kiss of life. He stood and walked for the oiled road with Porter beside him.

As they walked down the road and away from the Larue home, Porter chuckled softly and took Uzziah's arm as if he would hold his hand, but all he did was hold his arm.

"I knew this was meant to be," Porter whispered.

"That why ya fired yer pistol and scared those wagon hosses?"

"Yep," was all Porter said as he continued to cling to his new best friend.

6

Immanuel had waited for the return of the doctor's granddaughter from boarding school. He had even asked if he could be permitted to pick her up from there when the time came, but the doctor had just looked at him, and somehow Immanuel knew exactly what he was thinking. At some point, he had even wondered why this man, this doctor—yeah, they took a Hippocratic oath, and yeah, it started with, *"First do no harm,"* but it sure didn't say anything about taking a man into your home and exposing your granddaughter to a deflowering from such a man. *What*, Immanuel wondered, *could convince a man to do such a thing?* He swore if he had a granddaughter, he would never allow such a thing, but it didn't keep him from dreaming about the girl/young woman just about every night.

Then, during one of those dreams about the young woman, he heard a voice, and it sure sounded familiar. He was looking at the young woman get dress, which was about the same as having an undressing dream in reverse, but this voice, he had to turn away from what he was seeing, and there sat Uzziah, he was dressed like some fundamentalist pastor, all in black and wearing a flat-brimmed hat, and he was reading scripture and this is what Immanuel heard, "*A man of noble birth went to a distant country to have himself appointed king and then to return. So he called ten of his servants and gave them ten minas. 'Put this money to work,' he said, 'until I come back.'*

"But his subjects hated him and sent a delegation after him to say, 'We don't want this man to be our king.'

"He was made king, however, and returned home. Then he sent for the servants to whom he had given the money, in order to find out what they had gained with it.

"The first one came and said, 'Sir, your mina has earned ten more.'

"'Well done, my good servant!' his master replied. 'Because you have been trustworthy in a very small matter, take charge of ten cities.'

"The second came and said, 'Sir, your mina has earned five more.'

"His master answered, 'You take charge of five cities.'

"Then another servant came and said, 'Sir, here is your mina, I have kept it laid away in a piece of cloth. I was afraid of you, because you are a hard man. You take out what you did not put in and reap what you did not sow.'

"His master replied, 'I will judge you by your own words, you wicked servant! You knew, did you, that I am a hard man, taking out what I did not put in, and reaping what I did not sow? Why then didn't you put my money on deposit, so that when I came back, I could have collected it with interest?'

"Then he said to those standing by, 'Take his mina away from him and give it to the one who has ten minas.'

"'Sir,' they said, 'he already has ten!'

"He replied, 'I tell you that to everyone who has, more will be given, but as for the one who has nothing, even what they have will be taken away. But those enemies of mine who did not want me to be king over them—bring them here and kill them in front of me.'"

When Uzziah was finished reading, he turned to Immanuel and pointed at the page of scripture he'd read from, then closed the book and looked away.

Immanuel awakened from the dream and his body was covered in sweat, and his nightshirt soaked. He got up, tore off the wet nightshirt, and scoffed.

"What the hell could that mean?" he said out loud. There was no answer because he was in the bedchamber which the good doctor had given him, then he sat down, not because he was sick, but because he realized the monies he'd taken from his pa, Patrick Gass, all that money was about gone. He hadn't even looked at investments or anything.

That morning at breakfast, Dr. Gâteaux was surprised when Immanuel walked into the breakfast solarium room with the sun warming it nicely, even though it was well into November. Immanuel gathered from the array of things which had been put out a modicum of things which he thought he might like. A bagel, cream cheese, some salmon, which the doctor had told him was good for his heart, which was feeling much better, then poured himself some of the good and strong French roast coffee, left it black, then sat down beside the doctor, who was looking at him in an exaggerated manner.

"Yes, I am joinin' ya fer breakfast, though, I wished ya had biscuits, but ya don't."

"I can have Andre make us some," Dr. Gâteaux said.

"Nah," Immanuel said and bit into the bagel, which he'd put some of the salmon on, "What's a good investment in this town, anyway?"

"Well," said Dr. Gâteaux as he rubbed his chin, as was his custom when he thought, "Real estate would be my first choice."

"What 'bout shippin' and imports, and such?" Immanuel said, speaking through his mastication. The doctor looked away, such manners, or was it lack thereof?

"Wars will come, they always do, sir, and when that happens, if your ships, or the ships you have invested in, run up against the enemy, and who can tell who that will be at the time, well, your investment gets sunk or your cargo gets pirated, and then where are you? But, and this is a very important *but,* investing in land, and this town, well, Monsieur. You can never go wrong."

After breakfast, he went into his room and into the back of his sock drawer, where he pulled out the last of the money that his father had given him. It wasn't that much. What he'd won on the boat, well, most of it, had been stolen from him, and what he had left now wasn't enough to buy a coffeeshop. There was only one thing he could do, take this money and turn it into a small fortune, and the only way to do that was to gamble. In anybody else's mind, that was not a foregone conclusion, but in Immanuel's it certainly was.

He left the house, he'd been taking small walks, and he hired a hack.

"What's the best place to make a killin' in this chere town?" Immanuel asked the driver as he was getting in.

"Well," the youngish man said in a French accent. "Do you like cards or horses?"

"Ya got horse races here?"

"Do we? We have three tracks. The Jackson Course, the Eclipse Track, and the Metairie Race Course."

"Take me to the best one in your opinion," Immanuel said, and he got in and the hack took off. The driver took the next street traveling northwest, and before they even got there, Immanuel could hear the cheering of the crowd. The hack pulled up outside a two-tiered grandstand where literally thousands of people were sitting and enjoying the afternoon racing.

He paid the driver, got himself a racing bulletin, then walked out and peered up at the grandest sight he had probably ever seen. Women dressed up as if they were going to balls, men in their best dress suits, parasols and ivory-topped walking sticks. Now, this was a crowd where money could be spent. They had just announced the next race, which would take place in twenty minutes. The crowd's attention was directed over to the stables, where the ponies in the next race would be on display.

All the way over there, and there was a pressing crowd, Immanuel kept wishing Uzziah were here. He couldn't think of any thoroughbred that could outrace his chubby friend's horse, and that was with Uzziah on him! What if one of those skinny small jockeys got on Shadow? What would happen then?

He went to the fence where the trainers were bringing out the horses, and the second horse out was a dead-ringer for Shadow. In fact, Immanuel looked around, thinking that he would spot his partner of nearly ten years. Perhaps he'd come back and was going to win them all sorts of monies by entering Shadow in this race. But Uzziah was nowhere to be seen, Immanuel nudged a gentleman beside him, and asked a question. "Do you know the name of that black stallion, sir?"

The man looked at Immanuel as if one of the rabble had asked him a question, whereupon Immanuel pulled back the right side of his coat, revealing a new pistol he'd bought.

"Oh well, yes, of course," the man stuttered, "That's Stygian the Great."

A light went on in Immanuel's brain. He had read Greek mythology, of course, in translation, and he remembered the River Styx. Styx was a goddess, and when the Greek gods had their war and Zeus won, he ordered all oaths to be sworn by her. It was the River Styx that was crossed on the way to the Underworld.

So, he need not see another horse, if there was a God, and by God, if Uzziah had taught him anything, there certainly was, then God himself had brought Immanuel to Metairie Race Course for the third race, and there was the black horse named Stygian the Great, and hadn't Immanuel almost died on the way to New Orleans? Hadn't his partner left him to die alone, and now there was a horse that looked like Shadow, and had a most similar name, and all of this was running through his head as he almost ran to the betting windows.

The lines were medium, not long, and it didn't take long for Immanuel to be standing in front of a man who took all bets.

"I'd like to place this all on Stygian the Great," Immanuel said.

"How much is it?" The man looked down at the pile of bills which Immanuel had pulled from his pocket.

"Just count it and place it all on Stygian the Great!" Immanuel reiterated.

As he was counting, and there was quite a bit there, after all, Immanuel was placing every last cent he'd taken from his sock drawer, all the money that was left of what his father, Patrick Gass, had given him, the man at the betting window spoke up.

"Ya know why he's called Stygian the Great, don't you?"

"No, why?" asked Immanuel.

"That horse is one of the biggest jokes around the tracks in New Orleans. Why it's rumored if he loses this race, he'd be dog food by mornin'!"

Immanuel reached out and took hold of the pile of money the man was counting.

"What!?!"

"Didn't know that, did ya?" the man at the betting window asked. "Wanna place a different bet?"

Immanuel was about to take the money back. What was he thinking? Then a couple passed him, and the woman who was beautiful beyond belief said, "Well, he opened the door, and I wasn't going to go in there, it was positively Stygian!"

There were signs, and then there were signs.

"No! No, place it all on Stygian the Great," he said.

"It's your money, but it's a twenty-to-one shot, buddy."

"Fine, fine," Immanuel said, looking after the young couple and admiring the back of her hair and the fine shape of her figure, "All on Stygian the Great."

He walked back to the grandstands almost in a trance. He had bet every last cent of what his pa Patrick Gass had given him, and if he lost it all, he would be like the servant in the Bible, but worse, he wouldn't even have any of the King's money left.

He climbed into the stands, and his heart wasn't quite up to going as high as he wanted. He sure wished he had brought his spyglass with him. He settled into a seat about five rows up along the walkway on the first tier. He could see fine from there.

It took about another ten minutes before the horses were lined up, and then, they were off!

It was like a nightmare in which no matter how fast you run, the monsters are right behind you. It seemed to Immanuel that Stygian the Great was perhaps the slowest horse on the track, perhaps in the world, and by the time they made the first turn, he was last—dead last.

He was about to tear up the ticket stub, which would attest to his wastrel nature, when on the back straightaway, Stygian the Great made a move. It wasn't the fastest move in the world, and the jockey still wasn't using the quirt on him, but he wasn't last anymore. He was in the middle of the pack, and then he was two-thirds through it, and the crowd had picked up on what was happening, as they rose to their feet.

The woman in front of Immanuel had on such an

enormous, fluffy hat that his view was blocked. In a false gesture of cheering, Immanuel raised his arms and waved them, taking off the offending hat. The breeze caught it, and it was gone!

The woman turned around and looked at Immanuel. She, too, was beautiful, but he simply shrugged as it had been an accident, then they both heard the roar of the crowd, and looking, they saw Stygian the Great passing the leading horse, and they weren't even at the clubhouse turn.

Well, Immanuel had seen this before. The jockey had had the horse break too soon, and he would tire in the straight and another horse would win. This was probably Stygian's way to lose.

And yet, the beautiful black horse kept pulling away, it was like the other horses weren't running, and the crowd, regardless of what horse they'd bet on, liked what they saw.

When Stygian the Great crossed the finish line, he was nearly twenty lengths ahead of second place in the field. The crowd had gone wild, and many were tearing up tickets that they had purchased on other likelier horses, and some were hugging each other, and that's when Immanuel did a reality check.

Looking down at the ticket, he saw in black and white that he had, indeed, placed a huge wager on a horse which was twenty to one, and now, he placed the ticket in his inside vest pocket and, saying nothing to anyone, walked calmly to the ticket window.

When he got there, the line was really short, not many had bet on Stygian, and not many had won. He got in line and then heard a voice behind him.

"Fine, you knock my favorite hat to God knows where and then you get in line in front of me!"

When he turned around, he hadn't remembered the woman in front of him as the woman with the younger man who had actually said the word, *Stygian*, but there she was. Beautiful, even more so since she had lost her chapeau.

"If I may be so bold," Immanuel began, "You were beautiful with the chapeau, but without it you are ravishing!"

The younger man at her side bristled and was about to bow-up, when she spoke to him.

"Stop it!" she said to the younger man, then to Immanuel, she said, "You'll have to excuse my brother, he's overly protective, and father will not let me go anywhere without him," she said, giving Immanuel the most gracious smile.

Voices in the back of the line spoke up, "Move up, sir, if you will!"

Immanuel turned and caught up the distance that had grown.

"Did you win?" she asked him.

"Well, I'd rather not say," Immanuel whispered.

"That much?" she whispered back to him.

"Where's the best place for me to have lunch with you?" he asked her.

"Why?"

"We can go there and take the opportunity to count my winnings," Immanuel said with his most seductive smile.

"I don't think it's a good idea," her brother said, he'd been eavesdropping.

"And that makes it perfect," she said, looking at her

brother, "We shall go to a place I know of, despite my younger brother's objections, and he can tattle me out when we get home."

"Can we make a detour before lunch? It's right here at the race track," Immanuel asked.

"Most certainly," she said, as Immanuel stuffed every one of his pockets and she cashed in her ticket behind him.

They walked to the stables, and on the way, she took his arm, and he was delighted.

The brother said something, and she turned quickly and said, "Shut up, Richard." To both of their amazements, he kept quiet.

"Can ya tell me where Stygian the Great is stabled?" he asked a stable boy.

"Just follow the crowd," the boy said, cleaning up the messes that horses make.

There was a crowd, but it wasn't extensive, it drained away fairly quickly, and Immanuel walked right up to the man that he figured was the owner.

"How much?" Immanuel asked the man.

"For what?"

"Stygian, how much for the horse?"

"Well, he's finally won and I don't—"

"He's never won before and ya've got the winnings, and he'll probably never win again, ya know it was a complete fluke, right?" Immanuel said, looking down at the little man who was dressed rather nicely, then he added, "I know he was headed fer the glue factory, sir, I know!"

The man whispered something in Immanuel's ear, and he got out one pile of cash and paid him.

"I'll need a bill of sale," he told the former owner of Stygian.

"Of course, of course," he said, rushing into the office and coming out with the proper paperwork, which he filled out and signed, and Immanuel signed behind him.

"I'll pick the horse up this afternoon," Immanuel told him, and the three of them turned and walked toward the street.

7

Uzziah kept working at the quarry, and he didn't mind it at all. Hannah had told him when they sat on the porch one night all about the prophet's plans and what the temple would look like.

"Ya know, I have the worst time trying to see things like that in my mind," he had admitted. He loved listening to her talk, but envisioning something like the Nauvoo Temple was beyond his mental abilities.

"What time is it?" she asked him.

"Almost eight o'clock," he said, snapping his chronometer closed and placing it back in his vest pocket. He had earned enough money that he'd bought more clothes and given the ill-fitting ones back to Porter, who complained that the seat in the pants he'd loaned Uzziah had been stretched beyond their limits. Now, wherever Uzziah went, he would tip his new Latter-Day Saints' hat to the ladies, and he was glad-handing every deacon and bishop in the valley. When it became known that Ephrem Larue had accepted Uzziah's request to court his daughter, well, the whole town opened up to the both of them.

Hannah was sitting there thinking when her pa walked out on the porch.

"Would it be all right if we visited the prophet tonight?"

Her pa looked at his pocket watch, "I think it'd be fine, but don't stay too long."

They walked down the street hand in hand.

"I just love being seen with you, Uzziah."

"I know."

"Vanity is a sin, you know?" she said, looking up at him.

"But joking isn't," he said, chuckling with her.

"You always know how to get me, don't you?" she asked shyly.

"Now, and forever," he said, and they stopped and kissed each other there in the street, but she broke it off.

"More of that when we're married forever," she said, smiling.

"Forever?"

"When we speak to the prophet about our marriage, he'll explain it all to you. Here we are."

They walked up the path to the porch, and there was still activity in the house. Many lamps were lit, and you could hear the laughter of children and parents before you got on the porch.

Uzziah knocked, and Joseph Smith opened the door, "What a lovely surprise!" he nearly shouted, "Emma, look who's here."

Emma came from the kitchen, wiping her hands on an apron. She was an attractive woman, but really not a match for the prophet in looks.

"What do we owe this honor?" she asked, and Joseph laughed.

"That's one thing I will always love about this woman, her humility," the prophet said, and she smiled and went back to the kitchen. Uzziah looked after her, but she did not return.

"We'd like to see the plans for the Nauvoo Temple," Hannah said, casting her eyes downward when she spoke to him. He put his hand under her chin and raised her head so that he could look into her eyes.

"You, Hannah, need never look down when you are speaking to me. Why, the loveliness of your face alone is enough to keep me captivated."

"The plans to the Nauvoo Temple?" she said softly, smiling.

"Of course, come this way," the prophet said, and he led them into his study on the eastern side of the front of the house.

He opened the big front drawer on his giant oak desk and pulled out rolled-up parchments which had been banded together with wang leather. Untying the wang leather, he spread the architectural plans out, placing a paperweight on one corner, the Bible on another, the Book of Mormon on a third, and taking his pistol from its holster, he finished securing the plans.

"Do you remember my explanations?" he asked Hannah, who did not look down again as she spoke.

"Of course, who could forget?"

"Leave them there on the desk when you're through, and I shall have Emma put them up," the prophet said, and he left the office.

There was a lamp lit on the desk, and it was the only light in the room. The moon was nearly full, and its fullness was shining in from the east, and the room was very pleasant.

"Okay, now, instead of just telling you, I can speak while pointing out the features of the temple you're helping to build. Sit down in the prophet's chair and I will stand and give a lecture," she said and giggled. He joined in but it was a deep chuckle.

"Now, first you must know that the prophet has received new revelations since we began this temple for Nauvoo," she said.

"I thought all his revelations were back when he was a young boy of seventeen?"

"No, no, he continues to receive words from God from time to time. For example, the basement here"—she pointed to the second, which was to be the basement—"will have a baptismal font in it for the baptizing of the dead—"

"Excuse me, did ya say the baptizing of the dead?!?"

"Yes, the dead, isn't that exciting?"

"They don't dunk the dead bodies in the font, do they?" Uzziah asked.

Hannah shrieked and put her hand to her mouth, and the prophet appeared in the doorway, evidently, Uzziah noted, he wasn't that far away.

"Everything's fine, Uzziah just said something funny," she explained, and the prophet was gone again.

"I think he likes you," Uzziah said.

"Well, of course he does. My pa is high in the church, and he was there when I was born. There was even a rumor, if you hadn't come along as you did, that I might be one of the prophet's wives," she said, turning scarlet.

"No kiddin'," Uzziah said and not much liking the sound of that.

"Anyway, that won't be now, will it?"

"I should hope not."

"It would have been a privilege, though, that's what my pa says. So, down there in the basement, there's going to be—well, it's already there, perhaps you've seen it?"

"No, I just deliver the stones for the buildin'," he said.

"Well, it is gigantic and it sits on the backs of twelve wooden oxen and that's where chosen members, Latter-Day Saints, get baptized in proxy for those who have gone on."

"Proxy?" Uzziah asked.

"Yes, you know they take the name of the dead person and they stand in for them so they can be baptized."

"Oh," was all Uzziah said, but his head at this point was spinning.

"It's also where the prophet received the revelation that marriages within the LDS Church are eternal!"

"Ya mean, when we gets married, we'll be married in heaven, too?"

"Yes!" she said and hugged his neck. "Isn't that wonderful!"

"Well, I guess I never thought about it. I mean till I met you, sweetheart, I didn't think I were a marrin' man," he said, and she kissed him sweetly.

"You are the sweetest man I ever met," she said, then she added, "The last of the rituals the prophet received as prophecy is the ritual of endowment."

"Ain't that when someone gives ya property or money?" he asked.

"My pa explained it to me. It's when we get prepared for kings, queens, priests, and priestesses in the afterlife."

"Ain't just goin' to be with God enough, goin' to heaven?"

"Sure, but we Latter-Day Saints believe that if we reenact the story of biblical creation, and the story of Adam and Eve, and in the process, we get washed and anointed, and we get special heavenly garments to wear—"

"How can we wear something from heaven till we get there?" he asked, but she was so caught up in what she was saying, she simply continued.

"We get a new name which we will use in heaven and are taught words and signals, or signs, by which we are able to pass through angels who are guarding the path to heaven."

"It don't say nothin' 'bout that in the Bible, St. Paul don't say nothin' 'bout this kinda stuff," Uzziah almost protested.

"Of course not, these revelations had to come later, when the time was ripe and ready," she said. "You'll have to get your endowment a year after you been baptized."

"So, ya already have a special name that ya can't tell me?" he asked almost pleadingly.

"I do, but you'll get one and then you'll understand," she said, then added, "Let me finish telling you about the Nauvoo Temple, okay?"

"Sure."

"At each corner of the temple, there will be a rectangular column. There will be thirty of these in the temple with a moonstone at the base, and a sunstone at the top of each one."

"That all means what?"

"Well, the sunstones have two hands above and to the sides of each one, and they are holding a trumpet, which is to designate the dawning of the Restoration. And each sunstone has a starstone above it, and all that's from your Bible."

"Where in the Holy Bible?" Uzziah was getting a bit anxious about what he considered all this mumbo-jumbo.

"Revelation 12, 'clothed with the sun, and the moon under her feet and upon her head a crown of twelve stars'," she quoted. "It's all so wonderful, isn't it?"

Well, he thought, *he was helping to build the thing, and he loved her, and if she believed it was wonderful, then it was, right?* But in the back of his mind, he could hear a man's laughter, and he was fairly sure it was Immanuel's.

"Yes, darlin', it is wonderful," he said as the prophet walked in right on cue.

The next day at work, he was deep in thought, not so much that he would risk his life again, but Porter noticed.

"Whatcha thinkin' now, philosopher?"

"Have ya seen the plans on this chere temple?"

"Well, sure, I was one of the first to see 'em after the

prophet had them drawn up, in fact, he helped in the drawings, why?"

"Tell me what ya think of all the sun, moon, and starstones?"

"They're pretty, I know that," Porter said.

"And how 'bout this endowment thing?"

"Yer overthinkin' it, Uzziah, really. Do ya know any club in any big city that just lets ya in without ya havin' a password or a club handshake, heck even the Masons got that, don't they?"

"My grandpa was a Mason," Uzziah suddenly remembered.

"And did he tell ya all the secret stuff that went with being one?"

"No, course not, that's only fer those in the fraternity of Masons."

"So, God don't have no special handshakes and signs to get into heaven?"

"Well," Uzziah said, "it says in Isaiah, 'For my thoughts are not yer thoughts, neither are yer ways my ways, declares the Lord, As the heavens are higher than the earth, so are my ways higher than yer ways, and my thoughts than yer thoughts.'"

"Yer overthinking everything, young son," Porter said, and was reminded once again of his best friend. "Ya loves Hannah, right?"

"I do," he admitted and smiled broadly.

"Then, ya gots to 'member what yer Saint Paul says in the first letter to the Corinthians, 'For the unbelieving husband has been sanctified through his wife, and the unbelieving wife has been sanctified through her believing husband,' right?"

"Right," Uzziah said, thinking about how Porter knew his Bible as well as he did the Book of Mormon.

"So, stop overthinkin' it, okay. Just take the ride and all will be revealed in the end," Porter said, slapping Uzziah on the shoulder.

8

The luncheon at the lady's favorite place wasn't that far from the Metairie Race Course. Her brother, Richard, was sullen and acted like he might be all of eight years old, when he was easily that plus ten years. She was a delightful luncheon companion and laughed at the drop of a hat. Immanuel had never imagined that he was that entertaining. And yet, each tale he told her of what Uzziah and he had done in the mountains, with the Injuns, him being buried in New Mexico, and on and on, well, you'd have thought he was a regular Oscar Wilde.

He didn't mind, even if he was exaggerating. When she threw back her head and laughed like that, her skirts came up and he saw a delicious thigh or two and the decolletage, which was pushed between her arms when she leaned forward, made him want to take a bite, at least.

He kept looking at her younger brother Richard and looking back at her, she got the idea.

"Richard, do go get me another drink, will you?"

"Why can't he get it for you?" he asked.

"You haven't been listening, the man has heart problems, now go!" she ordered.

Once he'd left, Immanuel leaned forward and whispered to her.

"Dr. Gâteaux's house on Chartres Street, do ya know the place?"

"Yes, of course, it's a lovely house, why?"

"I have a room there," he said as he put his hand on her knee underneath the dress.

"But what of your couer, your heart?" she asked, touching his hand on her knee.

"I have almost completely recovered. This would be the final step."

"I've always wanted to help a doctor," she said, smiling.

"We could take a ride on Stygian, the next day," he said, still smiling his best smile.

"Well, I could tell Papa that I'm staying with my girlfriend, Margaux," she said, smiling back. "Here he comes with that damned drink," she said, taking his hand off her leg.

He put them in a carriage and watched them drive off, her gloved hand came from the carriage window and waved to him, or at least he thought it was a wave. He wondered if he had been too forward, not to her, but for himself? Was he ready? Would he collapse in a pile on his bed and expire? He had heard of men dying in bed, when *le petite mort* became *le grand mort*, but he wasn't exactly in the market for trying it out.

He was in such a good mood, flirtatious behavior always put him in a good mood. What was more wonderful than reenacting the Garden of Eden, the biblical creation with the Eve of your choice? The apple he wanted to give, Evette, that was her name, yet that apple already had a worm in it, and maybe she'd suck the worm, you never could tell with a woman, but she looked the type—what did the French call it soixante-neuf? He thought that was the word, it was mutually benefiting when done in that manner, and if, and it was a big *if*, then he'd see what happened. The only problem was the good doctor. The doctor stayed in the back of the house, which was some distance from his room, but they might make noise. He could ask her to be quiet, but what fun would that be?

When he'd said goodbye to Evette and Richard, who was absolutely thrilled to be out of their company, Immanuel imagined Richard going home, closing his bedroom door, and playing with his toy wooden soldiers, Engarde! Or something like that?

He walked back toward the stables, where he saw the owner of Stygian the Great saying a sorrowful goodbye to the horse. He was holding the horse's head in his arms and crying. *Ludicrous*, thought Immanuel. All that the man had was an English saddle, and he put it on for Immanuel and he mounted up. Sort of like sitting on a ton of dynamite with a postage stamp between you and the explosion. The man started in again with the horse, and Immanuel rode away, shouting back over his shoulder, "Hug your money!"

When he got to the Chartres Street address, he rode around to the back, where there was a small stable, and to his surprise, the good doctor was back there.

"Where did you get that magnificent creature?" Dr. Gâteaux asked.

"He won a race for me, so I bought him," Immanuel said as he dismounted. Holding the English saddle in his hand, he asked, "Do you ride English?"

"Certainment!" Dr. Gâteaux said, and Immanuel hung the saddle on one of the pegs in the stable.

"It's yers, I prefer western," Immanuel said.

"Merci beaucoup!"

"Not a problem, maybe we can go for a ride sometime," Immanuel said, then, in a manner he was unaccustomed to, he decided to be upfront with the doctor.

"Would you mind if a young lady dropped by to see me tonight?"

Dr. Gâteaux raised his eyebrows, then smiled, "Not at all. At least it won't be my granddaughter."

It was Immanuel's turn to smile, and he thought, *Well, not this time,* then decided to ask the doctor a professional question, "Has it been too soon after my angina pectoris?"

"You have been satisfying yourself in other ways, have you not?" he asked in his quite frank French manner.

"Well, yes, but—"

"Don't worry, I can't hear anything in the back of the house, but if that manner has been successful for you with no chest pains during and after, then the actual of sex should be fine," he said as he put away the saddle soap and rag, and started to walk back to the house, "By the way, who is she?"

"She was at the races with her brother, Richard—"

"Evette, yes, I know her, and the disgrace she has brought on her family, she's almost unmarriable now, but I suppose in such a metropolitan place as New Orleans, that no longer matters," he finished and walked away.

Immanuel rubbed down Trevor first and said some things to him which reassured him he was still his favorite horse, but Trevor's eyes kept roving to the big black, and he knew, deep down, he knew. The next trip they took, he would be packing the luggage.

Immanuel started humming, then singing, one of his favorites, "Oh beautiful for spacious skies, for amber waves of grain..." He had a deep baritone voice, and the melody carried throughout the neighborhood. Dr. Gâteaux was sitting on his back porch with a glass of Burgundy, and he hummed along with Immanuel, he, too, like the tune. The doctor had come from France many years ago, and at first, New Orleans just seemed a bit of Paris in America, but as he got to know the country—he loved to travel—he began to appreciate what the founders of this great country had done. As the song wound down, the doctor stood up on his porch, put down the wineglass, and put his hand over his heart.

9

Nearly the whole town of Nauvoo was present at Uzziah O'Bannon's baptism. He was being helped into his white baptismal clothes by Porter Rockwell, and the church they were using before the temple was complete was packed.

"I never seen this many at any baptism," Porter said, listening to the hubbub in the congregation, "but then again, it ain't every day we get a Gentile like you to be Mormon!"

"I done been baptized, I told Joseph, but he said it ain't the same, but I figured one immersion is as good as another," Uzziah said.

"Well, just wait till ya see how long the prophet holds ya under, it'll be a test of yer faith," Porter said with a straight face.

"Yer kiddin' right?"

"One feller had to be revived he was held under so long," Porter said without smiling.

It was time. A Deacon came and got Uzziah and Porter went back out front to sit with his family.

When Uzziah walked down into the baptismal font, he looked out, and he could see Hannah sitting there smiling like there was no tomorrow. He had decided he would stay under as long as it took to be able to be with that woman.

When the prophet dunked him, Uzziah refused to be lifted up when Smith tried to bring him to the surface. Uzziah figured that was a test, and he was going to pass. Once again, Smith tried pulling the big man up, but Uzziah stayed under.

"Porter, get up here!" the prophet had said, and Rockwell jumped the wall of the font, splashing the prophet, and the two of them were able to bring Uzziah to the surface.

Uzziah was gasping like a fish out of water.

"What was that all about?" the prophet asked in a whisper.

"That was all my fault," Porter whispered back, and Uzziah basically shouted, "Did I stay under long enough!?!"

The congregation loved it. They started hooting and hollering, and even at the party at the prophet's house later, all they could talk about was how a Gentile had shown them all up, determined to go be with Jesus at his baptism.

Hannah was good-natured about it, but when the crowd thinned, she pulled Uzziah aside. "Did you and Porter have a bet on how long you could stay down?" she whispered to him.

"No, hon, I just like the water," he lied, and she smiled.

Uzziah and Hannah Larue were to be married in the morning. He had visited with the prophet about the wedding and understood that his endowment would not be for a year following his baptism in the LDS Church.

The day of the wedding, Uzziah had wanted Immanuel to be his best man, but there was an automatic stand-in for him in the form of one Orin Porter Rockwell. Porter's little girls scattered the flowers down the aisle, and his young son, Orin Jr., carried the pillow with the rings on it.

The service had been conducted by the Prophet Joseph Smith. It was done on the first floor of the temple in Nauvoo, which had a ceiling of sorts on it, the floor joists for the next level. It was early in winter, and the temple was heated by many charcoal fires which vented nicely through the unfinished portions of the walls and ceiling.

It was the first wedding done in the Nauvoo Temple, and another great honor for the Larue family. It seemed that Uzziah had brought nothing but honor and happiness with him when he'd come to Nauvoo. They had wanted to go some place special on their honeymoon, but had decided that it would wait until the spring when the country roads were neither muddy from the rains nor icy from the wind and snow.

The biggest surprise of all was the little cabin, which was completely furnished and had two bedrooms and three fireplaces in it. The Larue boys, along with Porter Rockwell, and a lot of other Latter-Day Saint men had built it in their spare time, which must have been at night, Uzziah imagined, since they were always working on the temple. Regardless, when they thought they would be driven to the Larue house and live in Hannah's bedroom, instead they were driven to their new cabin, which was over the hill and in a secluded spot away from most of Nauvoo.

Uzziah loved it. It made him think of what his cabin might have looked like in the Rockies if someone had just taken the loving care to make it look like that. He was determined, if, by chance, and he couldn't imagine what those chances would be, if, by chance, he was forced back to the mountains, he would replicate the interior of this cabin up there. Who knew? Maybe the discrimination against the Mormons would grow into a war—after all, wasn't that why Joseph Smith had petitioned the Illinois governor so they could form their own Mormon Militia?

Whatever, perhaps he and Hannah could get away from all that hatred and move into the Rockies, but he knew he was trying to combine two different worlds—the world before he was a Mormon and had met the love of his life, and the world since he had met her. He actually felt a certain amount of guilt about thinking about those things, but he was, above all else, a practical man, a practical mountain man!

Uzziah was given two weeks off from his endeavors in the quarry, and when it came time for him to go back to work, it seemed that perhaps only two days had passed. He loved her, she loved him, and whatever else happened in that new cabin, it was blessed with a lot of energy which came from that love.

The building of the Nauvoo Temple went on into the winter. They cut stone and hauled it to the site with the snow flying, and then, as winter was about to break into spring, Hannah drove a buggy up to the quarry to bring Uzziah some hot soup and freshly made bread.

Ever since their wedding, she had excelled as a wife and doted on her husband as if he were the prophet himself.

They were sitting in the carriage and the top was up, and the sides were drawn to keep out the cold, but the wind wasn't blowing, and with the heated bricks she'd brought along under the big horse blanket, they were cozy as could be. She hardly ate any soup, her stomach had been acting up, but she delighted in watching her big man eat. She had said to him once that it was almost like being in a bear's cave and being privileged to see how a wild animal ate.

He wasn't so sure that was much of a compliment, but he let it slide, as far as he was concerned, Hannah could do no wrong.

As he was sitting there, sopping the last of the soup with the last of the fresh bread, he looked at her and she was glowing.

"Ya look different," he said, turning his head to complete the look of the wild animal, as if it did not understand.

"I am different," she said softly and grabbed the hand that had just relinquished the empty soup spoon.

"How?" he asked and wanted to look at her hair, maybe she'd fashioned it differently, but that wouldn't be like a good Latter-Day Saint woman.

She took his hand and placed it over her stomach,

and for just a second, he thought she wanted to have sex in the carriage in the middle of winter. Well, he was game. He started to move his hand down to that puff of hair where he'd found so much pleasure, but she pulled it back to her stomach.

"I don't know who you think I am, but I'm different here," she said as she patted his hand that was on her stomach.

Well, as most women of that time knew, men weren't the brightest candles on the Christmas trees, and she knew that, too, but it was the way she looked into his eyes that finally got through to him, she hoped.

"Yer hungry, and I done ate all the bread and soup, I am so—"

"Uzziah!" she had shouted, and even the men in the tent who were having their lunches and some of them by their women, looked out the parted tent flaps at the nearby carriage.

"What?"

"I'm with child," she whispered, and immediately tears began to flow from his big blue eyes, and she began to cry with him silently as he held her ever so close.

"This is the greatest moment of my life," he whispered into her ear, and she hiccupped, and they both began to chuckle.

From that moment on, he refused to let her bring him food at lunch. Finally, the weather got so bad, the snow so high, and the temperatures so low that for nearly two weeks, they sat in their cabin that Ephrem had given them as a wedding present, and they did simple things like sew, well, she sewed while he read the Book of Mormon again, and he cleaned all his weapons. Well, he started to, but the smell of the gun oil had bothered her so badly that he ended up doing most of the cleaning in the barn, where he got to visit with Shadow and Jenny.

The donkey brayed as if she were complaining that he had spent so little time with them, and he tried to explain about the coming of the baby and how life was moving on, and that he loved them, but their days in the mountains were done for, and this was their new life.

Shadow seemed happy when Uzziah left, and Jenny, too. Well, he had fed them extra oats and poured molasses on them, even though he had to heat the bottle to get it out.

Before he left the barn, he began to think of Immanuel. Uzziah hadn't spent much time away from Hannah since they'd discovered that they were in love and that God wanted them to be together. Their love-making was special, and when they weren't actually doing it, and they did it a lot, well, he didn't like the idea of anyone else ever having her. She was his, according to the Mormon ritual of marriage in this life and in the life to come. But something tugged at his heart, and when he sat still long enough, he knew it was his best friend, Immanuel James Jones.

He wondered if the man had spent all his new pa's money and disgraced himself, and he wondered what kind of trouble he'd gotten himself into that would have required his help, but he, Uzziah, was nowhere to be seen. It made his heart melancholy, that's what it did, and he rushed back into the house, through the blowing snow and the darkening night, so that he could tuck those feelings away in a place that couldn't touch Hannah and their coming baby.

10

Immanuel did not die the first time he actually made love after his—what were they calling it now?—his heart attack. He almost wished he had. Evette, it turned out, was more interested in his money than his passion, and though he had enjoyed his time in bed with her, they parted ways, and he was glad that he would never have to see her brother Richard again, ever!

The Christmas season was upon them, and Immanuel was having new thoughts about Dr. Gâteaux's granddaughter. He must have asked too many questions about when she would be returning, and how long she would be staying, for the good doctor had written a letter to Immanuel's father, one Patrick Gass.

The doctor was not proud of what he had done, but he'd written a letter to the man and invited him down for the holidays in New Orleans. Perhaps with his father and, if he was right, Immanuel's stepmother, who happened to be French, with the two of them in attendance during his granddaughter's Christmas break from school, then the granddaughter would be safe. In any case, he had done it, and one night when he and Immanuel were having supper, there came a knock at the door out front, and the servant girl had come back with two people in tow.

It was dark in the long hallway with only minimal lamps lit, and it wasn't till they entered the dining room that Immanuel looked up and there stood Patrick and Harriet Gass. The fork was halfway to his mouth, for he had surmised that the guest would only be for the doctor, and quickly he put the fork down and embraced his father.

"Patrick, what are you doing here?" Immanuel asked. His father did not answer that question, but turned and introduced the woman next to him.

"Immanuel, my son, I'd like you to meet your stepmother, Harriet Somme Gass."

Immanuel started to take her hand and kiss it, which was the rage in New Orleans, but he was surprised when Harriet, his new stepmother, took him into her arms and embraced him with as much passion as you would expect from any French woman. Well, she thought, he was much better looking than his father, and good-looking men are not a dime a dozen. Besides, she was closer in age to Immanuel than she was to her husband, and again, she was French!

"I am," she began in a slight French accent, and Patrick always accused her of turning it on and off when she so desired, "so very, how do you say"—oh my God, she was really putting on a show for Immanuel—"thrilled to meet the man that my husband fathered so many years ago," she said, not breaking from the hug, but keeping her arms slightly around him and leaning back so much the better to see his handsome face.

"Shall I call you mother?" Immanuel asked.

"Heavens no, we're closer in age than your father and I," she said, and she and Immanuel burst into laughter, and Patrick was already regretting having brought her along.

"Andre," Dr. Gâteaux shouted into the kitchen, "bring two more plates, please."

"If you are my guests, and you are, then you will join us for dinner, please."

Their food was brought, and Harriet sat right next to Immanuel, and he was having thoughts about his stepmother, which he was sure were unholy to say the least.

She was adorable and had a lot of knowledge about New Orleans, and she and Dr. Gâteaux would often break into long French conversations, which Patrick and Immanuel were not privy to.

In short, she was thrilled to be there. When the dessert was brought in a tres leches, which was fabulous, the men waited for Harriet to finish, and as she unpacked with the help of Gâteaux's servants into their rooms, the men adjourned to the wraparound porch out back and smoked cigars.

"So, Immanuel, what investment opportunities have we invested in—huh?—shipping, imports, exports, what exactly?"

"None of those, Pa, none of those," Immanuel said, playing the cat.

"Then, you have wasted my money!?!" Gass accused Immanuel, and Dr. Gâteaux and Immanuel broke into a good-hearted laughter, which was about to make Patrick mad, when Gâteaux spoke up.

"Can you see the lights in the distance?"

"You mean those, over your walls and to the north?"

"Yes, precisely, well, other people may own those houses and businesses, but your son was very wise, and all that property that they sit on now belongs to you, Patrick Gass."

"What?"

"Your son is wise beyond his years, and those twenty square city blocks are now landlorded by you, Monsieur."

"How many acres is that, son?" Gass asked.

"Eighty acres, Pa, close to downtown New Orleans," Immanuel said.

"There's a very nice hotel in that acreage, and the top floor has been cleared out for the new owners of the land it sits on," Dr. Gâteaux said.

Harriet had finished putting things away in their rooms and was standing there listening.

"We have to move already?" she said, perplexed, and the men laughed.

"No, darling, I'll explain later, but son, this is amazing, what you have done," Gass said.

"Without Dr. Gâteaux's advice, it wouldn't have been possible," Immanuel admitted.

"But I didn't give you that much money," Gass admitted.

"Come to the stables with me, I have something to show you," Immanuel said.

Harriet was thrilled to stay on the porch with the doctor, and they spoke in their native tongue about the town, no, the city of New Orleans, which was at that time, the fourth largest city in the world. She asked about the culture, the theatre, the opera, and the social scene, and by the time Patrick and Immanuel had gotten back from the stables, she had made up her mind.

"Patrick, Patrick, we must move here, permanently," she said, getting up and putting her arms around her husband and his new stepson.

"I was thinking the exact same thing, and Immanuel could stay on and manage all the property for us, and Monty and his wife could come visit in the winters, and all the other children, too."

Everyone was in agreement, extraordinary, really! Harriet was laughing and holding onto Immanuel like he was her anchor. Patrick had been handed a brandy by Gâteaux, and so too, Harriet and Immanuel, and they were toasting the Gass empire in New Orleans, which would be run by none other than their long-lost son, Immanuel James Jones.

The brandy tasted like acid to Immanuel, and it was good Napoleon brandy. The dream—at least the one his parents and Dr. Gâteaux had for him—was a nightmare. He was beginning to dislike city life even more than when he had lived in the mountains. His dreams were filled not with money, women, and fame, but with the Ponderosa pines whispering in their heights, and he couldn't help but think of Abooksigun sitting up in the land of the vapors, listening to the melting pots which were talking to him. These people would have thought that that particular Algonquin Injun was crazier than a bedbug, but Immanuel knew that it was Abooksigun's way of taking care of his soul.

They were all sitting on the wraparound porch and

drinking and laughing, and he didn't like the looks he was getting from his stepmother. His pa Patrick was not picking up on it, and the whole idea of walking, or even riding around parts of the city of New Orleans and collecting rents and mortgages made Immanuel sick to his stomach. What had he stepped in that he would not, could not get off the bottom of his boots? They were celebrating his entrapment, and he was feeling sick, very sick.

"You'll have to excuse me," Immanuel said. "I don't think the Vichyssoise agreed with me," he said, and when he looked at his stepmother, she winked at him and he turned away. Surely, there must have been something in her eye? Surely!

He went to his room and locked the door. He wasn't sure if he was just crazy or what, but it seemed necessary. His head was spinning, and all he could think about was Uzziah up there in the mountains, about to go through a winter on his own. What was he thinking about? He was already going through such a winter, and without his partner.

He got out of bed, and down on his knees, he had never done this in his life. Well, he had prayed when he was buried six feet under in that grave in Nuevo Mexico, but that was different, and he was supine. There was no looming death in front of him, no lid that held way over any amount of soil he could dig his way out of, but this casket, this enclosure of a society which was closing in on him, weighed as much as life itself.

"Father"—he'd heard Uzziah call God that—"I don't want to be here, I guess I don't want to be here any more than my Savior wanted to be on the cross, but surely, this isn't the life you intended me to live. Surely, the mountains, the wild animals, life among men who know the traps of civilized man, these wilds are the ones I am meant to live in, these surroundings are the ones in which I am meant to be! Please, give me a sign that this is your will. I know I will disappoint my new pa, but most of all I don't want to disappoint my partner, Uzziah. In Jesus's name," he said and rolled into the bed, and was fast asleep.

It must have been early morning, way early morning, but there was the largest rat in his dream, which was scratching at his window. He didn't think Dr. Gâteaux had rats, because he had an army of cats which slept in the stables and patrolled the house nightly. So, what was that noise? It had stopped, and he rolled over against the wall and was nearly asleep again when he heard the front window in his room being raised ever so gently.

He hadn't stopped sleeping with his pistol under his pillow, it was a habit that was hard to break. *Safety right here, under your pillow*. He reached his hand under and could hear the footsteps of someone coming toward his bed. He whirled in an instant and cocked the gun!

She screamed, but was wise enough to put her hand to her mouth. The house was enormous, and their rooms were near where Gâteaux slept. No one heard. He lit the lamp by his bed, and the thin chemise dropped off her body. She had been blessed with good breeding. She was amazing looking, with firm, large breasts and nicely formed thighs, and hardly any stomach at all, but she was Harriet Gass.

He hadn't taken the gun off her.

"Will you please put the gun down?" she whispered.

"I should spank you," Immanuel said, and realized that wasn't what you said in situations like this.

"Yes, please," she had responded and walked even closer to the bed.

He couldn't exactly scream, but this was his father's wife, and yes, she may be French, but even within French society, there are morals and upbringing.

"Get out!" he sibilated as he walked to the door he'd locked and unlocked it.

Her face turned immediately 100 years older. Well, it fell, shall we say, and whimpering, she grabbed up the sheer nightgown and slithered quickly from the room.

He relocked the door, sighed, and leaned against it. He would rather have faced an angry griz!

The next morning, he joined them in the solarium for breakfast. They were all there, chatting amicably about something in French. Perhaps she was telling the good doctor about her night of trying to get into her stepson's bed. Who knew? He didn't speak French, and he didn't want to!

Patrick seemed very glad to see him, and the two of them talked even though Harriet never stopped gibbering away in French to the doctor.

Finally, he turned to his new pa, Patrick Gass, and he leveled with him.

"Pa, something happened last night," was all he had started out with, and the conversation Francais, ended immediately. Harriet grabbed her napkin to wipe her mouth, but Immanuel was sure she was ready to cry.

"What's that, son?" Gass asked.

"I actually prayed to God about my situation here in New Orleans, and I'm fairly sure I got an answer just a few hours later," Immanuel said, and when he looked at Harriet, she was shaking her head *no*, very slightly.

"Well, you must tell me, I love it when God comes through like that," he said in a jovial manner, as if Immanuel, himself, were joking.

"I'm goin' back to my mountains," Immanuel said, never taking his eyes off Patrick Gass.

Gass looked down at his plate of Eggs Benedict, and then back up to his son.

"Son, I am amazed you've made it this long. Why, after I came back from the expedition, all I wanted to do was to get back to that wilderness. Most of my journeys to find you after I'd heard from that Black Robe was a mere subterfuge to simply breathe that air again," Gass said, and his eyes filled with tears.

At that moment, Immanuel realized that his pa, his new pa, was an honest man, maybe the most honest man on this earth. He had just admitted that when he went looking for his half-Mandan son, it was really only to get back to where the magic was.

Immanuel reached right over and grabbed Patrick Gass and hugged him tightly.

"You're givin' me my mountains back, it's the second time you've given me life," he whispered in Patrick's ear.

11

The winter was mild, they said, but there was plenty of snow. As yet the temperatures had stayed fairly warm for a winter in southern Illinois. The second-floor walls were going up and the Prophet Joseph Smith had been on the site many more times than in the beginning. Uzziah liked to see the man looking upward toward the very heavens which the Nauvoo Temple seemed to be reaching toward.

He and Porter were taking turns going from one man's house for lunch to the others. Hannah was getting big. Uzziah guessed he just hadn't paid much attention to a woman's belly. He had been there and conscious when at least eight of the last eleven were born to his ma, Rahab, but who looks at their mother's belly when they're with child. He certainly got an opportunity to see Hannah's belly. The amazing thing to Uzziah was how Hannah glowed. She had always been an attractive, even handsome woman, but being with child, she absolutely glowed—she was now truly beautiful.

One morning, when she was doing her hair in the only mirror in the house in the bedroom, Uzziah stood in back of her and whistled softly.

"What?" she had asked while looking at him in the mirror.

"The beauty which I am beholding."

"Beauty! I am as big as a cow—a cow with calf—I might add, and you are only seeing what you want to see," she said as her hands did marvelous things with her hair as she pinned various sections up and the nape of her neck was exposed.

Uzziah couldn't resist, he kneeled down with his hands on his future. Surely, the child was more than that, it was the third party in this family of how many he knew not. He could feel the baby kick as he nuzzled his nose and beard along her neck and kissed it gently.

"Uzziah!" she falsely protested, "You know what that does to me."

"Why do ya think I'm doin' it?"

"You're getting me to feel indecently," she said, the little hairs on the back of her neck standing up and her breathing became more rapid.

"What's Joseph said 'bout that?"

"No one would dare ask him!" she said, her hair fixed and looking Uzziah into his eyes in the mirror.

"Well, I don't think anythin' we does as far as how we feels is wrong, do you?"

"I know you don't—that was you two nights ago who lifted my nightshirt and helped yourself, wasn't it?"

"Ya know it was, and ya didn't protest, not one sign of protestation."

"I was still sleeping—"

"Un-huh, it was all Uzziah's goatish tendencies, weren't it?" he asked as she leaned back and pulled closer to him.

"Now, we are dressed, dawn is coming, and the day has begun," she said, looking at him from under her scolding brows.

"Okay."

"Now, tonight, when I'm incapacitated by slumber, such advances will be met with an entirely different outcome," she said, kissing him long on the mouth. "I can't imagine kissing you without a beard, it would be like eating eggs without salt!" she said as she got up and slipped past him into the larger portion of the cabin.

Uzziah had all three of the fireplaces going, even the one in the spare bedroom. She thought it a waste, but who knew when this new life was going to be upon them?

"We're goin' to Porter's fer the noon meal, see ya tonight," Uzziah said. "Every hour away from ya is torture, I swear."

"Please don't."

"Just a 'pression, sweet, just a 'pression," he said, kissing her on the forehead and going out the front door, heading for the warm barn.

Uzziah kept a small woodstove going in the barn, and most Latter-Day Saints thought he was crazy, but they hadn't lived in the Rockies, where your animals were the only thing that separated you from death.

Shadow greeted Uzziah with his usual enthusiasm, and Jenny started braying. All she could think about was her stomach.

Uzziah threw hay into their oversized stalls, and he also fed the milk cow. He had milked her earlier that morning and already taken the milk with the cream rising to the top inside the house, and put a piece of cheesecloth over it to keep out the bugs. The horses never bothered him in the early morning, since they had the schedule down pat. Shadow and Jenny would stay quiet when Uzziah was milking, and he knew that was the way of things in his pa's barn. It was like the horses and other critters knew that milking time was almost sacred. But it still puzzled him that when he was throwing the hay and grain for the cow, neither of the other two protested. He guessed they knew their time was coming—probably the reason Jenny made such a racket when he came in before going to work.

He picked up a little bit more hay for Shadow to take with them to the temple grounds. The workers had built a lean-to for their animals, and Uzziah always threw the last of Shadow's hay when he got to work. Without the hay, they couldn't stay warm, and they were certainly hayburners.

The work that day was fairly easy, as the walls went up, the stones got narrower as they tapered upward, and what they were gathering from the quarry now were stones of a lesser weight.

When they rode over to Porter's for lunch, the children were doing homework, almost all the LDS children were home-schooled, and men kept that in mind when picking a wife. She must be someone of intelligence who could transfer that knowledge on to his children. The job was obviously made easier when there was more than one wife, the load and the intelligence could be divided.

But Porter was basically a serial monogamist. His wife, Luana, was his only partner, and their three children were doing whatever exercises she had given them, even when they saw their pa and Uzziah, and they sort of squealed to be released, Luana spoke up. "Stay on task, and when that is completed, come to the table."

Uzziah was amazed that they did just that. Except Emily, who had finished her work, showed it to her mother, then went and hugged first her pa, then Uncle Uzziah. The children in Nauvoo had started regarding Uzziah as an uncle to all of them. As he rode down the street, he'd hear some child shout out, 'Uncle Uzziah!' and he never failed to stop and talk with the child, or at least wave and shout back if he was hurried.

He had come from the mountain's way out west, and he would tell them harrowing stories of his adventures with grizzly bears, bad hombres, Injuns, and stampeding buffalo. Most of the children had never even seen the humped back Buff, and their imaginations were set afire with Uzziah's stories of high adventure.

Once the prophet had come by that summer, when Uzziah was in the middle of one such story—it concerned the buffalo run when one boy was the buffalo runner and the other jealous boy, had been crushed by the falling buffalo. The prophet stood there and listened to the last of the tale, and when Uzziah was through and the children ran off, the prophet walked over and sat on the same stacked wall that Uzziah was seated on. The fountain in the middle of Nauvoo could be heard in the background.

"Do you really think, Uzziah, that those are the sort of stories which should be told to children?"

Uzziah thought for a moment then answered.

"That there story was about jealousy and the regrets that children have when they do not pay attention to their parents, so, yes, most of my stories have redeeming moral value because the men who lived those stories, myself and my partner, Immanuel, were all good men."

"I admire your old partner's name, Immanuel, almost wish I had that moniker. *God with us*, really!" the prophet said, then slapped Uzziah on the knee, stood, sighed, and looking up to heaven, he mouthed the words, "Thank you, Father," and was gone.

Emily had lingered over her pa and was hanging onto his neck.

"Child, I know ya love yer pa, but help me get this mess of lunch on the table, please," Luana said.

Emily sighed, kissed her pa on the cheek, and went to help her mother.

They had fried children, collard greens which they had hung in the root cellar, mashed taters from the same cellar, and hot cobbler. Uzziah barely felt like going back to work. And sure, hoped Hannah hadn't planned a big supper. He would have to fake his hunger, which he never found hard to do once he got started.

Then, it hit Uzziah that he should go check on Hannah, but he knew she was having some friends over to help her sew a quilt, and that meant that she wouldn't be alone, so he forgot about it.

They left to go back to work, and Uzziah thanked Luana profusely and kissed all three of the kids on the head, but Emily held onto Uzziah and kissed him back on the cheek. She sure was one sweet girl.

They worked the rest of the afternoon, and the snow had started to fall about an hour before they knocked off, and what the heck, they knocked off earlier than usual. No one was around to tell them they couldn't, and most of the work was done as a tithe to the church, so it wasn't like they were going to get paid less.

Uzziah rode Shadow in a gallop to the cabin on the other side of the Nauvoo Plaza, and when he pulled up, he saw her shadow moving within the house, and immediately relaxed—everything was as it should be. He tucked Shadow into the barn with the braying of Jenny filling the space. She did not understand why she wasn't able to accompany her two friends. He threw hay for all three now, Jenny, Shadow, and the milk cow that Hannah called milk cow, well, there were some animals that didn't need naming.

The supper she fixed him was lighter than usual, and he thanked the Father for that. He was nearly always hungry, and the meatloaf allowed him to eat what he wanted, and the scalloped potatoes tasted just fine and cheesy. She apologized for not having the energy to fix dessert, but Uzziah told her he was fine with what she had fixed.

They read in the parlor together for the last time on this earth. She was reading *The Pilgrim's Progress* from *This World to That Which is to Come* by John Bunyan. Uzziah had looked at it, and it was a Christian allegory which was considered at that time to be a significant work of religious literature.

He was reading *Poor Richard's Almanac,* and he was most interested in the weather predictions, which seemed to repeat themselves after so many years. He was interested in the weather in the Rockies, and he wasn't sure why. He then went on to read some of the poetry, which he wasn't ashamed to say he admired. At one point, he was chuckling about a saying he'd read, and when Hannah didn't ask him what he was chuckling about, he looked up. She was sound asleep with her head to one side, just the sort of thing that usually gave her a neck ache, which he would have to massage out of her neck before she could go to sleep.

"Come on, darlin'," he said as he reached down and scooped her off her favorite easy chair. She moaned, but did not wake up, well, at least tonight, he would not have to massage her neck, and for that he was grateful.

He walked her into the bedroom where the fire was blazing, and the room was nice and warm. He didn't want to undress her, so he simply threw back the covers and laid her down, then brought them up to her chin. He untied the bonnet on her head and pulled gently as he took it off. She opened her eyes and sleepily said, "Love you."

He was going to tell her he loved her too, but her eyes closed immediately and she started snoring. That was a good sign. He didn't undress either, and just laid on top of the covers, and they went to sleep like that. Her promise of his mischief would have to wait till another night.

In the middle of the night, the fire had died down, and he awoke to her moaning. At first, he thought she must be sick, but when he rocked her gently by moving her back and forth in the bed, she stopped.

It was later, and this time, the moaning was more urgent. He reached beneath the covers and her dress was wet. When he pulled out his hand, it looked like it was covered in black paint. He got up and went to the fire, throwing logs on, and in the up blaze, he saw that his hand was covered in blood. He threw back the covers and the bedsheets were soaked around her.

He ran to the barn, and without saddling Shadow, rode to town and got the Mormon midwives, who showed surprising agility in getting from the beds to their carriage. He raced ahead of them and lit lamps in the bedchamber after making sure that Hannah was still breathing, and she was.

They dismissed him from the bedchamber, and dressed Hannah in her nightgown. He, having built up the fire in the parlor, paced up and down in front of it. He could hear this and that, and from time to time, one of the midwives ran out to either boil water or get more rags. The rags they were bringing from the bedroom looked like they were dressing a deer in there, how could that much blood come from one woman?

It wasn't long after that that he heard a furtive cry as if a rabbit had been caught in a trap, then it turned into the muted squeal of a newly born baby. He burst through the door into the bedchamber, and what he saw, he would never unsee. The bed, all of it, was soaked with blood. Blood was dripping from the end of her side and they were wrapping a small object in swaddling clothes. He started to say something, but the warm bundle was thrust into his arms, and he went over by the fire to keep the child warm.

Hannah's eyes were rolling in their sockets, and then he spoke. "What's wrong?" he asked simply.

"She's getting ready to be with the Master," one of them said, and he wasn't sure that's what was said, but then he felt a shudder in his arms, and when he looked down, the baby boy had stopped breathing. He tried breathing into the little body, and he could get the chest to rise and fall, but the heartbeat never resumed.

That was when Hannah awakened and, looking over at him by the fire, holding their baby, she asked, "How's our baby?"

"He's perfect," Uzziah said, letting her know in two words that they had a perfect baby boy.

Hannah hung on for a while longer, maybe an hour, until the baby in his arms was cold as the stone he had gotten from the quarry.

Then, in a burst of energy, she sat up and held out her arms for the child. As Uzziah moved forward, her eyes rolled back into her head, her arms dropped back down as she convulsed on the bed, her back arching, and arching as if she would break her own back. Then, she fell back supine on the bed, dead and nearly purple in color, her mouth caught craggy in the energy of trying to survive.

They placed the body of Hannah on the wagon, wrapped in the bloody bedclothes, and when they reached for the dead child, Uzziah turned away from them and walked to the barn.

He heard the wagon leave with the midwives and the dead body of his wife, Hannah. He lit the lamp in the barn and, for the first time ever, Jenny did not bray but stuck her nose out to smell the swaddled thing in Uzziah's arms.

Shadow circled in his stall and kicked at the sides while the milk cow lowed.

Uzziah placed the bundle down long enough to saddle Shadow, and he let Jenny out of her stall. The night was cold, but she would be fine. He rode at a walking pace all the way into town, and instead of Jenny following, she rode ahead and brayed their arrival. By the time they had made the city of Nauvoo, all the residents were out on their porches or standing on the boardwalks, dressed in their nightclothes with jackets pulled firmly around them.

Uzziah rode, looking straight ahead. He'd tied the reins to the saddle horn and had the baby wrapped in both his arms as if he was trying to keep it warm.

The townspeople did not disappoint, they cried and wailed, and the men ran out to touch Uzziah's leg or arm, or part of his saddle. He rode all the way to Nauvoo Temple and, leaving the braying Jenny and Shadow in the barn, he walked right on in and carried his dead son to the altar. When he placed him there, he fell to his knees, and clasping his hands together, prayed that the God of us all, the Maker, Sustainer, and Redeemer of us all, would point a finger down and raise this smallness to life.

"Talitha kum," the prophet said as he kneeled beside Uzziah. Uzziah forgave him, he knew it was a boy, but what did Joe know? The words were from the gospel of Mark, and they were said over the dead body of a little girl, but whatever. It meant in English, "I say to you, little girl, get up."

Then the two men hugged in their kneeling and cried together.

Many years later, when Uzziah heard of the

prophet's death, he would cry again, knowing that the man had many faults, as all men do, but when the hoof hit the trail, Joe Smith was a regular guy, and didn't deserve to be shot down by a mob like a rabid dog.

When Uzziah got up, he took the dead boy from the altar, and the prophet stayed kneeling in prayer. He walked from the temple and rode to the morticians.

He entered the backroom, and the mortician had Hannah's naked body covered with a sheet. Uzziah took the body and, borrowing the midwives' wagon, he took Hannah home.

At the cabin, he carried her into the parlor and placed her in her favorite chair, the book she had been reading less than six hours ago was on the table, he picked it up and read, "*To go back is nothing but death, to go forward is fear of death, and life everlasting beyond it. I will yet go forward.*"

In the bedchamber, he threw the bloody clothes into the fireplace, and they smoldered then shot into flames, and walking back into the parlor, he laid Hannah's body on the coverlet, and then the unnamed body of the baby boy, whom he did not have the heart to speak a name for, beside his naked mother. They both, in the climbing flames in the fireplace, looked perfect. They were, they were perfectly dead.

He sat in the bedroom and watched them as the flames throughout the cabin died and the coals went out, and the house became as cold as death itself. He sat in the darkness and thought of *yet going forward.*

12

It was the winter in which Immanuel had sworn he would make it back to the cabins, and Uzziah seemed to be cooperating. It was cold, yeah, but the snow wasn't in drifts as he got off the paddle boat at Fort Mandan, or at least where the fort used to be. He stayed a night with his birth mother and his six brothers, and realized that these people were more of what he was made of than anyone back east.

They were told the story of Stygian the Great, but mostly, they thought Immanuel was a liar, and it was probably more likely that he had stolen the horse, which to the Mandan way, was just as good a story. He kept telling them what had really happened, but they were having a hard time imagining the grandstands, and thousands of people watching a horse race. Finally, Immanuel admitted he stole the horse, right from under a rancher's nose, and they were all much happier that he had come clean.

They wanted him to stay longer, and several of the brothers wanted to travel back with him to the mountains, but all they had to do was to think how cold it was by the Mighty Mo and multiply that by many degrees lower. They all settled into saying their goodbyes to him, and wanted him to know that he and Uzziah were welcomed whenever, wherever.

As he rode away, he did not look back because that was the Mandan way. When you leave, you leave.

It was still a good week and a half in good weather, and he wasn't sure how long he was on the trail. At one point, he saw a group of Injuns off to the south and east, but they paid him less attention than he paid them. The cold weather and threat of more snow had a habit of taking the fight out of everybody.

He didn't bother with smokeless fires, and would have killed anyone who even bothered him. Perhaps it was that shroud of death, that feeling he was carrying with him of losing the most important person in his life to booze and whores, the flint of his going, which drove before him a path that was not crossed and not even bothered.

When the Rockies came into view through the fog, he began to weep, but they were tears of thanksgiving that God, the God of Abraham, Isaac, and Uzziah, had allowed him this wondrous sight before his heart stopped again. He had been where most men would have wanted to stay in the warmth and bosom of wealth and security, but had left simply because, in his mind, those were the portents of death, maybe not now, but soon enough, a death that would come like a thief in the night and take the wonder from his lifeless body.

He stopped at Vrain Trading Post and was greeted by Jean Baptiste as if something was wrong.

"Uzziah dead, is that why yer lookin' at me like that?"

"No, no," Jean Baptiste had said.

"Then what is it, damn it!?!" Immanuel demanded.

"Your death is not far behind you," a Crow said to him in Crow.

Immanuel whipped his head around, and the Hawken came up as if the Injun, the Crow, was going to deliver that death.

"He's friendly," Jean Baptiste said.

"Do ya speak Crow?" Immanuel asked the owner of Vrain.

"Yeah, but ya know how it is, they speak in tongues of story, and nothing more."

"What you trying to say?" Immanuel asked the Crow.

"Your death is not far behind you," he said again, and left with his wife, little boy, and the things he'd bought from Jean Baptiste.

"It's probably his way of saying ya got more years behind ya than in front," Jean Baptiste said.

"Still," Immanuel complained, and he gathered the things which he had not wanted to carry from the Missouri River to this place, coffee, jerked meat, lucifers, another blanket, some flour, some flints, a new deck of cards and a cribbage board. He'd learned from the good doctor how to play and thought Uzziah would like the game, it was less a game of chance than just poker. He also got more powder and ball for the Hawken, got twice as much as he needed, figured Uzziah could use it and might be short by this time in the winter.

"Has it been this warm all winter?" he asked Jean Baptiste.

"Very strange, almost like it was waiting for you to get here," Jean Baptiste said in his thick Frenchie accent.

"Yeah, almost," Immanuel said.

"Whatever happened about them dodgers?" Jean Baptiste ventured.

"We dodged 'em," Immanuel said, picking up his change, his item of purchase, and not turning around as he left the trading post.

The trail up the mountain was a bit rough, there were sections that had frozen and re-thawed, and the going wasn't easy. He almost wished he'd stayed down at Vrain's till the next morning. It was going to be dark when he got there, but he thought about the surprise in Uzziah's eyes as he rode up and Uzziah emerged from his rebuilt cabin with the Hawken by his side, not trusting that it was a friend. He got Stygian up into a good dog trot up the hill, but had to let go of Trevor's reins so he could come the rest of the way by himself.

When he cleared the last rise before the cabins, he wasn't sure he was in the right place because there was no ambient light from the fires in the cabin to light the way, and then there they were.

They were just as they had been left when Uzziah, their two mountain man friends, Max and Frederick, who had not wanted the reward, had ridden away toward the settlement. How many years ago was that? Immanuel was trying to conjure up exactly how long, but the good doctor had told him sometimes, the angina pectoris had a habit of robbing memories.

The destruction was the same, but now covered with snow, not a lot, but some. He checked the tumblers, and they were still perched right where they'd left them. Good thing they left the coop door open, they could take care of themselves. Their cooing was the only greeting Immanuel was going to get, and a thousand stories of how Uzziah had died on the way back came storming into Immanuel's brain.

"I told ya, ya couldn't make it without me, damn ya, young son!" Immanuel yelled, and the tumblers flew from the coop and circled above in the blowing snow.

The barn was still in good shape, and he built the little stove up in there, which would not only keep Stygian and Trevor warm, but also himself. He guessed since Jesus himself had been born in a manger, that staying in a barn wasn't exactly that bad, but thoughts of the coming summers and winters without his partner made him remember the Crow's words, "Your death is not far behind you." *Damn Crow, speaking up when he should have kept his Injun mouth shut!*

He got the horses fed and made himself a pallet and walked back out to sit where he could look at the camp, the destroyed, or mostly blown up cabins, and his thoughts were fairly dark when he realized he was sitting right under the tree limb that they'd hung Benjamin from. He looked up, and the cut and unraveling rope was swinging up over his head. He stood and walked away, and looking back, remembered Uzziah's running jump to grab Benjamin and help him on into the next world.

For just a flash, he thought about just letting the

horses go and fixing up a better rope and riding the fastest horse he'd ever owned, riding it out with the noose choking the disappointment from him, but hell! He was made of sterner and certainly more courageous stuff. Tomorrow he would start building things back up, and worry about the rest later.

13

Uzziah awakened to the sound of hoofbeats. He looked out the side window of the cabin, and it was Porter Rockwell. He went to the front door and opened it.

"Brother, it's colder in here than it is outside," Rockwell said as he threw some wood on the dying embers. He picked up the jar of coal oil that was sitting beside the fireplace, and threw some on the wood, and it flared back up.

"Sit down," Porter said. "I got us somethin'," he said and went back outside.

When he came back in, he had a bottle of bonded whiskey. It wasn't Jameson, but it was tasty. What Uzziah loved about the man was his similarity to Immanuel. He didn't say anything obvious or say anything stupid, like, *Sorry 'bout yer loss.* They just sat in the front room and got toasted in front of the fire and didn't say a thing.

About two-thirds through the bottle, he spoke. "The prophet wants to talk to you after the funeral."

"Oh yeah?"

"Yeah?"

"'Bout what?"

"Who knows, maybe he's had another revelation," Porter said, and they both laughed. It was hollow laughter, and it ended quickly.

They went into the bedchamber, and Uzziah realized that Hannah wouldn't want Porter to see her naked, but Porter had a way of looking without looking. They got out Hannah's best dress, and everything that a lady Mormon would wear, and between the two of them they twisted her un-rigored body into all those clothes. Uzziah tied the bonnet back on her head, which he had untied the night before, and it was too much for him. He collapsed into Porter's arms and the two big men cried like babies. Then, they thought about Uzziah's son lying there naked. Hannah had made clothes for the child, and Uzziah picked out an outfit that looked good on the baby.

"We done had a stillborn, not quite the same, but amazing looking, ain't he, looks like he could just start breathing," Porter said.

They carried the two dead bodies out to the wagon that belonged to the midwives, and drove them back into town. This time, all that happened was a lot of hats coming off and bowed heads.

The prophet was at his house, and they drove the wagon there, and he was sitting on the porch all bundled up when they got there.

Inside his house were the Larues—all of them. Mrs. Larue, the next oldest girl, she was barely fourteen, the two Uzziah had saved in the fake runaway carriage accident, well, it wasn't fake, but it was sort of staged, and then the other kids. They were all fairly upset.

Hannah's pa, Ephrem, came forward and took Uzziah's hand and said something, but Uzziah didn't exactly understand. It sounded like *There's another one,* which didn't make any sense at all. What the hell did that mean? *There's another one*—was there another death in the town of Nauvoo that night?

The mother cried on Uzziah's shoulder, and the boy and girl he'd saved grabbed him like it was as close to their departed sister as they were ever going to get, and in truth, it was.

The prophet pulled them aside and, taking them out to his barn, there sat two separate coffins, one for Hannah and one little one for the little guy. Porter clicked up the horses on the wagon, and about that time, the whole town seemed to be gathered on the street in front of the prophet's home.

Inside the barn, they carried Hannah, and the prophet carried the child close to his breast.

They laid Hannah down in the fine casket, there was silk all around and a stuffed silk pillow. Uzziah imagined that must have cost a lot. They started to lay the baby in the small coffin, which was just as plush, but Uzziah stepped in and took the baby in his arms. The prophet thought it was only right that Uzziah wanted to lay the boy to his final rest, but Uzziah turned away from the little box, laid the baby boy in the coffin with Hannah, and moved her arm to embrace him.

The prophet looked at Porter, who just shrugged, then he looked at Uzziah as if he were about to speak, and Uzziah held up his hand.

"He belongs to Father when we lay him in the ground, but she never got to hold him. Now, he belongs to Hannah," he said, his voice breaking. He closed the coffin.

They walked in their best shoes and boots to the Nauvoo Temple, and the service that was held included music and singing as if the heavenly angels were singing, and Uzziah thought, *Those Mormons can let it out*!

They six shouldered the one coffin out to the consecrated ground that surrounded the temple, and Uzziah realized he would have to look at that grave as long as he was helping to finish the temple.

The prophet spoke over the grave, and for the life of him, all Uzziah could think of was the evening before this one, they had sat in their home and read together in peace.

Afterward, at the celebration in the temple of the resurrection and life, Uzziah was approached by Ephrem Larue, and he had Hannah's sister, the oldest sister now, with him. Her eyes were cast down as Ephrem spoke.

"She'll do her duty," Ephrem said.

And Uzziah looked at her as if maybe her duty was something concerning the funeral, he couldn't imagine what that would be.

"She can raise up children for ya in Hannah's remembrance, it's the right thing to do," Ephrem said, pushing the girl toward Uzziah and walking away.

They stood there at the *celebration* of her older

sister's funeral and the baby born alive, but then dying shortly afterward.

"How old are ya?" Uzziah asked.

"I'll be fourteen in a couple weeks," she said, sort of smiling at him, and he could tell she was trembling.

"Do you love me?" he asked her, and knew it was an unfair question.

She just looked at him as if it were a trick question.

"Forget loving me, don't ya have a boyfriend?"

"Hiram McKenzie likes me," she said and blushed.

"Do ya like him?"

"Well, sure," she said and grabbed Uzziah's arm, "but this is what my pa wants," she finished up and almost smiled a real smile.

"Look, this is between you and me, don't tell yer pa, okay?"

"Okay," she said as she got closer to the big mountain man.

"I think yer great, and will make somebody a great wife, but according to the prophet, yer sister"—he tried to say her name and he simply couldn't—"yer sister and I are celestial married, she'll be waitin' fer me in heaven, ya understand?

"Sure, I get it," she said.

"Did yer sister ever catch ya with somethin' that belonged to her?"

"Yeah," she said, remembering.

"What happened?"

"She got really mad!"

"Okay, we don't want any angry people in heaven, do we?"

"No, certainly not!"

"Good, yer swell, and I'm leavin' now, but don't

make like ya know that," he said as he kissed her on top of the head and walked away. Ephrem was smiling as Uzziah walked away, not knowing what they had said.

Uzziah walked over to Porter and pulled him aside as they walked out of the temple.

"Brother Porter, I am leavin'," Uzziah said.

"Kinda figured," Porter said and extended his arm the way Immanuel and the Injuns shook hands.

"I will never ferget our friendship, truly. Here's where ya can get in touch with me," Uzziah said and handed a folded piece of paper to Porter, who opened it, and then said, "Ain't got my glasses."

"It's okay, they can find me, no matter what," Uzziah said and embraced the man, who hugged him back. "Tell Luana how much she meant to me as a brother's wife," he added.

Porter was tearing up and shook his head up and down.

He watched as Uzziah mounted up on Shadow and headed for the other side of town.

At the cabin, Uzziah walked through once, got Jenny from the barn, and put the sawbuck on her back and the supplies he'd already packed. This was decided the minute Hannah had died.

As he rode into the sunset toward the west, he thought about how he'd have to rebuild the blown-up cabins by himself, but he would have Hannah's memories with him, and for the first few years, that would be all he needed.

MOHAWK GEORGE

1

The weather was cooperating on a lot of levels. Uzziah decided to travel due south, perhaps the climes would be better down toward the Missouri. It was cold, well, it was nearly into winter, and the Missouri was frozen in some places, well, near the shore, but then further into the stream it was still flowing toward its confluence with the Mississippi. He had thought about taking one of the big paddle wheelers, but the trepidation of the steamboat companies was getting frozen on the upper Missouri, and the passengers would then be subject to whatever whims the natives would have in store for them. The biggest deterrent to being bushwhacked by Injuns was the good old moving target. Instead, he packed up everything on Jenny and rode Shadow following the Mighty Mo.

It was actually easy sailing, so to speak, as far as Jeff City. That was the informal name for Jefferson City, which had been the capital of Missouri since 1831. It was right on the Missouri, and Uzziah decided he would stay there a while, just to pick up whatever he had forgotten and that eventually, he might need, and to take stock as to where he was, and how long it was going to take him to get *home.*

There was a hotel across the street from a saloon that served good food. He ate supper there, then crossed the street to the hostlers and put Jenny and Shadow away. The old man there liked horses, well, with a job like that, you'd better. He especially got a kick out of Jenny's braying, and before Uzziah had left, the old man was scratching her under her chin. He had a friend forever. He walked back up the street to the hotel to get a room. Once he was settled in, he went back across the street to the saloon to see what the local population looked like.

He was still in his Mormon garb, including his flat-brimmed hat. He ordered a beer and, leaning on the bar, took a look at everybody in the place. There were several men in some sort of uniform at the bar, and when he got a better look, a patch on their shoulders announced that they were guards at the Missouri State Prison in Jefferson City. One of the guards saw him staring and spoke up.

"What ya lookin' at, Moron?" That was one of the favorite ways for Gentiles to goad Mormons.

"Just lookin' 'round, friend," Uzziah said and went back to his beer. He had been smart and was packing a pistol under his broadcloth jacket, which hung down below the barrel of the gun.

"I ain't yer friend, Moron. That's what I's call all ye morons!" He spoke loud and looked around the saloon for some smiles, but everybody else was minding their own business. "Ain't ya gonna do nothin' 'bout me callin' ya a Moron?!" he insisted, having gotten no support from the other customers.

"Jake, forget it," the guard beside him said, probably the man's only friend. "Ain't no Moron worth gettin' in a scrape with."

Uzziah was in mourning, and he wasn't in the mood to have the religion of his dead wife, Hannah, and his unnamed son toyed with.

"Yeah, Jake, better listen to yer friend," Uzziah advised, and before Uzziah had finished the sentence, Jake had pulled his pistol and was wailing away at Uzziah. The man behind him went down holding his shoulder, the mirror behind the bar exploded into a million shards, and a bottle sitting on the bar exploded. Everybody was trying to get out of the way, then Jake's hammer clicked on spent cartridges.

"Well, I'll be," the man said, seeing that Uzziah was unscathed.

Uzziah drew his weapon slowly, and the two *friends* of Jake's scattered. Jake was hastily reloading his weapon, and still Uzziah's pistol hung by his leg.

"Whacha waitin' fer, he's a gonna kill ya," an old man yelled from the back of the bar.

"Get finished with yer reloadin'," Uzziah recommended to Jake, whose shells were falling on the barroom floor as quickly as they were getting into his weapon. Finally, he snapped the weapon shut and began firing off in the direction of Uzziah.

Truth be told, Uzziah was ready to be with Hannah. They had had a celestial marriage, and if this Jake was going to send him to her and his son, then so much the better for Jake.

Jake's firing was doing a great job of destroying the bar and the bottles behind it, and when again, his firing piece clicked on empty shells, the barkeep slid a sawed-off shotgun to the guard. Uzziah figured the barkeep had had enough destruction for one night and just wanted the Mormon dead. Jake picked the shotgun up, and Uzziah fired his first shot, which clipped Jake's right shoulder, where the tendon holding up the arm that held the shotgun was, and the scattergun clattered to the floor.

Jake bent down to pick it up with his other arm, and a voice came from the batwing doors. "Jake Heatherton, ifn ya pick that up, I'll kill ya," said a man with a star on his chest, who had just walked through the doors which were still swishing back and forth. Jake halted, and then the sheriff's deputy who had entered behind him put the cuffs on the wounded man.

"Damned Mormons!" Jake finally got the name right, at least. "Yer all gonna burn in hell fer the way ya believe."

Those in the saloon just couldn't wait to tell the sheriff what they had seen, and they all described it differently. "He just stood there, bravest man I ever witnessed," one man said.

"He only fired one shot, and that was when the shotgun got called into play," said another.

"I shouldn't have slid him my scattergun, but I got tired of seeing all my stock shot to hell," the barkeep said, then added, "He'll have to pay fer all the damages, won't he?"

Then it was just Uzziah and Sheriff Laurie sitting at a back table, both of them with beers, and since both were naturally laconic men, they had gone through half the mug before the sheriff felt obliged to say something.

"Where ya comin' from?"

"Nauvoo."

"Ya a Mormon?"

"I am."

"But ya carry a sidearm and drink?"

"Ever heard of Porter Rockwell?" Uzziah said.

"So, yer him, huh?"

"No," Uzziah said, laughing openly. "He's a friend of mine. My name's Uzziah Ferguson O'Bannon."

"Ya was tried for the murder of that Pinkerton, weren't ya?"

"That story got 'round."

"In all the papers," the sheriff said by way of explanation.

"Case was thrown out."

"So what ya doin' in Jeff City?"

"Passin' through."

"To where?"

"Rocky Mountains."

"Son, ya been hit in the head recently or something?"

"No, sir."

Sheriff Laurie looked around, and there were entirely too many ears on this conversation. "Come on over to the jail with me, would ya?"

"Am I arrested?"

"No, no, son. I'm Sheriff Buck Laurie, and we should have a talk, that's all."

Uzziah picked up the beer he'd been enjoying and downed the rest of it. Sheriff Buck Laurie was on foot, so Uzziah walked along beside the sheriff. When the sheriff looked back, five to seven men had exited the saloon and were standing on the boardwalk looking their way. *Why couldn't people mind their own business?* the sheriff wondered.

Inside the sheriff's office, the deputy, a boy not any older than seventeen or eighteen, had put the prisoner in his cell and was closing the door to where the cells were. Jake had had enough whiskey that he yelled as the door was closing, "Gonna get the Moron's testimony afore ya git mine!?"

Thankfully, the door to the cells was heavy and reinforced in case someone wanted to get at a prisoner. The sounds of Jake's yelling were muffled after that.

Sheriff Laurie just looked at the door, and taking off his holster, hung it on a big carpentry nail which was halfway driven into the wall behind his desk, and sat down.

"Swear, this job don't ever stop," he said, seeming tired and exhausted as he looked Uzziah over better in the lamplight of his office.

"Sheriff, Ma's expecting me to supper," the boy said.

"Yeah, yeah, go ahead, Willy, there ain't nothin' else to do," Sheriff Laurie said.

"My name's William Hart, but people sometimes call me Willy," he said to Uzziah as he stuck out his hand, and the boy and the man shook hands.

"Nice to meet ya, young son," Uzziah said and smiled for the first time since he got to Jeff City.

"Is it true what those men said—"

"Willy, yer ma's waitin' on ya," Sheriff Laurie reminded the lad.

The boy left and the sheriff chuckled. "That boy likes ya."

"I do believe yer right," Uzziah said.

"And, I ain't sure why I'm sayin' this, but I think I do, too. Any man that can stand fer twelve shots to be fired at him, and not even duck! And that shot as my prisoner raised up the Greener! I thought old Jake in there was a goner, but ya shaved his arm, and he dropped the damn thing, best shootin' I seen in a long time."

Uzziah just sat there.

"Yeah, well, I don't much like praise either, but I needs a man like ya, ya understand?"

"Go on," Uzziah encouraged him.

"Look, from everythin' I heard back at the Golden Owl, ya was tryin' to git yerself kilt, but it didn't happen, that so?"

"Maybe." Uzziah could not, would not admit to what he had been thinking.

"Ya said yer gonna go to the rocks in the west, right?"

"Uh-huh."

"This time a year?"

"Yep."

"Sueycide."

"Maybe."

"Ain't no maybe. Look, Jeff City's a good place to winter. The job, the one I'm offerin' ya, comes with a little house, ain't fer from here, I can show ya. Whatcha say, help an old lawman out, will ya?"

Boy oh boy, the things, the ideas, the concepts which were swirling around in Uzziah's head, he could hardly contain them, mostly all he could see was

Hannah's sweet face, and her lips were moving, he was a good lipreader, and she was saying, "Carry each other's burdens and so you will fulfill the law of Christ," it was from Paul's letter to the Galatians.

Sheriff Laurie's head dropped. When a man was silent that long, it usually meant one thing, *no*.

"Does the little house have a barn?" Uzziah said, standing up.

The sheriff looked up and his face changed from lost to saved in that moment, "Ah, sure, yeah, you bet," he said, getting up, strapping on his gun, and opening the door for Uzziah.

The sheriff followed Uzziah down to the hostlers, where he paid the man the full due, even though he protested. "Had a jenny like her once, were a pleasure to be entertained by her, no charge," the old man insisted, but Uzziah just put the money in the old man's outstretched hand. People say what they say, but their actions give them away.

Jenny brayed all the way to the little house.

"Is she always like this?" Sheriff Laurie asked, looking back and smiling at Jenny.

"Not always, but think she knows a warm barn is in her future," Uzziah said.

The little house was about the same size as the cabin that Hannah and Uzziah had occupied in Nauvoo. It was down by the Missouri, it flowed right by, but was up on a ridge, so floods would pass them by. The barn was almost attached, and the distance between the two was less than twenty feet, good for feeding in the winter snows.

The sheriff opened the barn and lit the lamp, and there were stalls, four of them, and a hayloft with hay.

"I harvested that, but part of it's yurin, ifn ya need it," Sheriff Laurie said while taking out his pocket watch and flipping it open, "Too late fer ya to meet the wife, but come in the mornin' and have breakfast with us, ifn ya will?"

"Where's that?"

The sheriff walked out and pointed down the road to a larger home with lamps blazing in it. "There she is, not more than a half mile away. We eats 'bout sevenish," he said, and stuck out his hand to Uzziah, who shook it.

"Ya done save my bacon, that's a fer sure," he said as he mounted up on his little roan and rode toward the house in the distance.

Uzziah went back in, took Shadow's saddle off him, and the sawbuck off Jenny, she brayed of course.

"Looks like we done found us a new home fer a while," Uzziah said as he climbed up, knocked down some hay, and threw it in the stalls. He looked around and there was a barrel of oats, and he threw some on top of the hay. Both of the critters looked at him with, he could only imagine, gratitude.

He took the lit lamp and walked the short distance to the closest door to the little house. It opened into the kitchen. It was fairly clean, which led Uzziah to imagine whoever lived there had just vacated. The bedroom had nice rope bedsprings, which didn't need to be retied. There was a bureau, and another lamp with oil in it by the bed on a night table.

He made sure all the doors and windows were closed, and he laid his bedroll out on the bed and got on top of the bed, much like the last time he'd laid down with his Hannah. Thoughts of her swirled through his mind—a picnic that they'd had next to the pond outside the heavenly saloon in Nauvoo, the chuck she brought when the weather was nice, and how they laughed about everything. The church services where Joe Smith was orating, and he wished he'd paid more attention, but his only thoughts then and now were of her—Hannah Larue. He went to sleep with a smile on his face and did not dream at all.

2

He was up way before it was time to eat at Sheriff Laurie's home. He looked down there when he went to feed the horse and donkey, and Laurie waved from a half mile away. He was up doing chores, too. Jenny was sleeping in the extra hay he'd thrown, and he looked around for a little stove which would keep them warm in the throes of winter. Surely, in a town the size of Jeff City, there was a store that would have one.

As he was fixing the interior of the barn, the way he liked to work a barn, he thought of all the destruction awaiting him up at the cabins. Immanuel would be doing what Immanuel did best, and he didn't expect that would ever change. He saddled up Shadow, and it was too early to go to the sheriff's house, so he rode back into town, and up and down the streets.

There were some soiled doves who waved to him. They were hanging their linens out and barely clothed, even though it wasn't warm. It made him cold just looking at how little they had on. He was surprised at his reaction to their bare flesh. They were flaunting it, and in the past, he would have gotten a bit aroused, but nothing like that was happening. He rode over to where they were smoking and dealing with their bedclothes.

"Hey, handsome, what's a Mormon doin' lookin' at nearly naked ladies?" the brashest of them asked.

"Ladies, I'm the new deputy in town, and I want ya to know, ifn any man lays a hand on ya like ya don't want him to, or aren't getting paid to let him do it, come and report it to me."

They looked at each other as if the Savior had just appeared and blessed them.

"Get away from here!" a burly man with a large pistol strapped to his side, and only in his shirtsleeves, yelled as he stepped from the brothel.

"I will not," Uzziah said, and the man pulled his weapon as a threat.

"I said—" the man started in, and Uzziah threw his tomahawk and knocked the gun out of the man's hand, cutting him some.

"What the!?" he protested as Uzziah jumped off Shadow, took some wang leather, and tied the man's hands behind him and tied his lariat around his waist. He jumped back up on Shadow and took off for the jail. The burly man lost his footing and was dragged through the mud with the soiled doves cheering in the background. Uzziah knew that most likely the protection for them was also their tormentors. The man finally regained his feet, and by the time they got to the main street, he was swearing a blue streak. Uzziah stopped Shadow and turned in the saddle.

"Ifn ya'd like to go to jail unconscious, that can be arranged," he said quietly.

The man looked at him as if Uzziah had lost his mind.

"You don't know who I am!" he protested softly.

"And I don't care," Uzziah said and continued, and whatever else the man had to say got lost in his trying to keep up.

When they got to the sheriff's office, Willy had the fire going and coffee on. Uzziah walked in with his prisoner, and Willy just stared.

"Well, open up a cell, young son," Uzziah said.

"That there's Pete Betz," Willy said in amazement.

"Well, see," Uzziah said to Pete as he undid the wang leather and took the lariat off his midsection. "There's always somebody to introduce us, ain't there?" he said, pushing Pete Betz down the hall toward the cells.

"Yer gonna regret doin' this, lawman," Betz said.

"I hardly doubt it," Uzziah said, opening the cell door and gesturing him to enter.

As he locked the cell, Betz continued, "Mr. Gongloe is gonna see to it that ya join the most recent of deputies up on boot hill," Pete said, smirking all the while.

"Well, I can't wait to meet yer boss, I'll just bet he's a peach," Uzziah said as he twirled the keys and walked toward the office.

When Uzziah got to the sheriff's house, it was half past seven, and he did not like to be late.

"We wondered where ya was."

"Sorry, I'm late, ma'am," Uzziah said to Mrs. Laurie.

"Call me Beth, please," she said, and was quite pleasant.

"What happened?" Sheriff asked.

"Got us a new prisoner," Uzziah said as he sat down across from the sheriff, and Beth passed him plates of sausage and biscuits.

"I waited to put the eggs on, how ya like 'em?" she asked.

"Over's fine."

"Some drunk in town? And what was ya doin' in town anyways?"

"Got ready fer breakfast early and decided to take a ride through town, arrested one," Uzziah said, taking a small notebook from his vest and reading the name, "Pete Betz—"

"What!?"

"Buck!" Beth said in a warning manner. "Mind yer heart," she added.

The sheriff just looked at Uzziah.

"My guess is, he's not a man to be arrested, am I right?"

"That boss of his is the bane to Jeff City, he's got his fingers in more pies, and they're all dirty—"

"Ya don't know that, Buck," Beth cautioned as she filled his plate with food.

"I do, and every time I get one behind bars, he's got his damned—'cuse me, darlin'—lawyer to get him out. What's Betz do this time?"

"Shall we pray?" Uzziah said, extending his hands to both of the Lauries. They took his hands and Uzziah began, "Father of us all, we thank ye fer this meal which has been so expertly prepared, and we pray yer protection over the sheriff and all his deputies. Bless this house and make it a sanctuary of rest for those who live here. In Jesus's name. Amen.

"Drew his gun on me," Uzziah said, filling his mouth with the luscious breakfast.

"Huh?" the sheriff asked, he'd lost the thread with the prayer and all.

"He drew his gun on the law and I arrested him," Uzziah said, and Beth had her hand to her mouth.

"Ya ain't dead!" Buck nearly shouted.

"Nope."

"Betz don't draw unless he fires."

"Knocked it outta his hand. Oh yeah, better get the Doc over there to look at his shootin' hand," Uzziah added.

"Ya shot it outta his hand?" Buck queried as he began eating.

"Nah, knock it out with my tomahawk," Uzziah said, and he touched the weapon, which hung by his right side. Beth looked down at it and moved her chair closer to her husband, the sheriff.

The sheriff looked at Beth, smiling. "Did ya hear that, knocked it outta his hand with his tomahawk."

"Yeah, dear, I heard."

"We got 'em locked up ain't goin' nowhere till after breakfast," Uzziah said, then added as he split open a biscuit, "Pass me the jam, Beth, is that blackberry?"

"Yes, yes, it is," she said as she passed him the mason jar.

They rode toward town and the sheriff spoke up.

"Look, sorry, I basically scolded ya fer what ya done, but Gongloe's had this town by the tit since he got here years ago. He's mostly respectable, but we sorta came to a truce after my last deputy was kilt."

"The man who used to live in the little house?"

"Yeah, Frank Sims, good man, but he was found gutted in an alley one night after he crossed Gongloe's men."

"Let me guess, since the so-called truce, he'd pushed the line over and over again, right?"

"Yeah, yeah, he has, how'd ya know?"

Uzziah kicked up Shadow a bit, and the sheriff did the same with his roan.

"It's the way of bullying, never changes, till it changes."

"What's that mean?"

"Gots to draw a line, then don't let him pass it," Uzziah said.

"Look, my law dog days are in their sunset years," he began.

"Don't worry, I'll do the drawin' and the not lettin' him pass," Uzziah said.

"Boy, ya got a death wish?"

"Yeah, I wish death would leave me and mine the hell alone," Uzziah said, and the sheriff didn't know what to make of that.

When they got to the sheriff's office, Willy was agitated. "They come by to get Betz, but I locked the doors and hid," he said.

"Good boy," said the sheriff.

"Who come by?" Uzziah asked.

"Gongloe, hisself," Willy said.

"Where's this Gongloe hang out?" Uzziah asked.

"Down the street at the Devil's Den," Buck said.

"I was at the back of that place when Betz threw down on me," Uzziah said. "I know the place, I'll go talk to him."

"Not without an army, ya won't," Sheriff Laurie said.

"Don't worry, I'll be fine," Uzziah said, and went out, mounted up on Shadow, and rode the three blocks to the Den.

The place was open even though it was barely eight thirty. And sort of crowded. Gambling was going on, a roulette wheel, a Faro game, and other poker games. Uzziah walked in dressed just as he had been in Nauvoo and right up to the bar.

"I needs to speak with Mr. Gongloe," he said to the barkeep, who looked down at the end of the bar, where a man wearing a low-slung pistol and hat walked the bar toward Uzziah.

"Who the hell are you?" he asked Uzziah.

"I'm the man that arrested Peter Betz," Uzziah said, moving his coat away from the 38 caliber Navy Colt hanging at his side. He'd admired Porter's guns so much he got himself one.

"Nobody calls him Peter," the man said, noticing Uzziah's move with his coat, and placing his hand down by his piece.

"I do," Uzziah said. "I mean, if it were good enough for his mama, it's good 'nuff fer me."

"Yer a wise ass, ain't ya?" the man said, and started

to draw, and Uzziah reached over and grabbed the holster, and the hand which had dipped into it.

The man tried to draw, but the gun was stuck in the holster. Several of the patrons were watching what looked like a man who was about to get a scolding from his papa, and they loved it.

"Where's Mr. Gongloe?"

"He's up chere," a voice said with just a trace of a Chinese accent.

Uzziah looked up to the balcony along the second floor, and this man had evidently stepped from a doorway and was talking to him.

"Ya Mr. Gongloe?"

"Yeah, come on up. Harry, stop acting the fool," Gongloe said, and Uzziah let go of the holster, his huge hand relaxing and Harry took his hand off his gun.

"Ya good?" Uzziah asked Harry.

"I'm a gonna git ya fer this," Harry whispered.

"Not today, yer not," Uzziah whispered back, as he walked right past the man who had tried to draw on him. Harry turned and faced Uzziah's back and Gongloe shook his head no. Harry turned back to the bar and hit it hard.

Uzziah walked up the stairs and down to where the man, who evidently was part Chinese and part Anglo, was standing beside the open door. He, Gongloe, was dressed in a very nice western suit, and had polished boots, black, and a golden vest which looked nice against his light blue trousers.

"Come in," Gongloe said, and gestured into his office.

The office opened up on the front of the Devil's Den and looked out on the street. There was another room off the office, and Uzziah could only imagine it might be Gongloe's bedchamber, but who knew?

The desk that occupied a great deal of the office space was huge and painted, well-lacquered black like a Chinese box. Behind it sat a chair which had also been lacquered black, and the cushions on it were black, too. The top of the desk was empty, nothing on it, and Gongloe sat in the chair and gestured to the chair in front of the lacquered desk. It was a regular pinewood chair with a straight back. Uzziah sat.

"Drink?" Gongloe asked as he produced a bottle from a silent drawer and poured himself three fingers in a glass.

"Some other time," Uzziah said.

"So, you drink?"

"When it's appropriate."

"Why the getup?" Gongloe asked as he sat back in his lacquered chair and put his feet out in front of him.

"It's the way Latter-Day Saints dress."

"So, you're a Mormon?"

"Among other things."

"Like?"

"The new deputy sheriff."

"And your name, so we'll know what to put on your tombstone," Gongloe said and took another sip.

"Oh, I won't be dyin' here," Uzziah said, and at that precise moment, a man stepped silently from the other door, and Uzziah threw his Bowie knife so fiercely that the big knife impaled him on the door. The door kept swinging with the dying man's effort as he tried to raise the gun in his hand. Finally, the gun dropped, and so did the man's head. He swung there like an ornament.

The knife had gone through the man and stuck out the other side of the door.

Gongloe had not moved, but he raised the glass to Uzziah and toasted the air.

"Uzziah Ferguson O'Bannon, and the next time that happens in yer presence, you'll be dead, too," he said.

"Fair enough, then, whenever you come in here, be guaranteed that this unfortunate accident, my men can be so hasty, well, it won't happen in my presence again."

"So, Mr. Gongloe, whatever arrangements ya had with Sheriff Laurie are no longer in force. You and your businesses will uphold the law, or be arrested for not doing so. Anyone who resists arrest will be shot dead, and that's that," Uzziah said as he got up from the chair.

"You talk a lot," Gongloe said.

"The ornament on yer door is, as the Chinese say, worth a thousand words," Uzziah said as he walked to the door, retrieved his Bowie, whereupon the man, whom he now recognized as Harry from the bar, fell to the floor in the bloody pool his body had dripped.

Uzziah went to the post office and talked with the postmaster there.

"Got any messenger services here in Jefferson City?"

"What ya mean, ya can send a letter anywheres ya just 'bout want," the older man said as he lit the pipe he had in his mouth.

"Yeah, but what ifn I needs to get a letter to someone faster than the mail?"

"We gots a couple of young boys who make money doin' just that, but it's pricey, I gots to warn ya," he said, blowing the smoke across the counter.

"This chere letter needs to get to Nauvoo as soon as possible," Uzziah said.

"Well, we send the mail on the stagecoach. The next one leaves at noon, probably be there by day after tomorrow," the man said.

"Okay, fine," Uzziah said, and went back to the sheriff's office to get some paper and a pen to write the letter with.

He rode Shadow down to the sheriff's office, and when he walked in, there was a man dressed in a suit, talking to the sheriff.

"We'll bail him out till the circuit Riding Judge can get here," the man said.

"No, bail for drawing a weapon on peace officers," Uzziah cut into the conversation.

"This is between Sheriff Laurie and the party I represent," the man said.

"Yeah, I know, Mr. Gongloe, right?"

"You know the man?" the lawyer asked.

"Yeah, we just got acquainted. Better get down there and help him arrange the funeral of Harry," Uzziah said.

"Harry Potts is dead?"

"He was the last time I saw him," Uzziah said. "Say, ya got a pen and paper I can use?" he asked the sheriff.

"So," the lawyer continued with the sheriff, "how much for the bail?"

The sheriff looked at Uzziah and shrugged, as if to say, *This one's yours*.

"Look, what's yer name?"

"Barrister Hawkenfield, why?"

"Listen up, Hawkenfield, as I just said, there ain't no bail on an offense such as drawing a gun on a peace officer. Ya did hear me say that, right?"

"Who's the sheriff here, anyway?" the lawyer asked.

"We's taken it together, Uzziah and I. He ain't my deputy like Willy, he's the sheriff, same as me. We's co-sheriffin' this town."

"That's absurd, you can't have two sheriffs!"

"Well, ya heard the man, right? He's sheriff and I'm sheriff, so that's the way it's gonna be, so no bail, git!" and Uzziah basically rushed him out of the office.

Once the door was shut, Buck Laurie started in, "This is so excitin' ain't it, Willy. Hell, we'll probably git ourselves kilt, but damn, I sure like standing up for once. Been sitting too long."

"The paper, the pen?"

The sheriff got the pen from the desk. "Inkwell's on the desk," he said, then pulled paper from the desk.

Uzziah sat down and the sheriff went over and poured himself another cup of coffee.

When the stage rolled into Nauvoo, nobody paid it much mind. It was mostly there for services which were not available in Nauvoo, and sometimes, letters which were posted at the post office were sent by it to places that those who now lived in Nauvoo used to live.

The man who drove the stage didn't much like being in Nauvoo, so without a word, he dropped the mail pouch at the post office and picked up the one that had letters to be mailed in it. No words were exchanged between the two men—one a Mormon and the other just another man afraid of something new and different.

Luana picked up the mail, hoping to have a letter from her aunt, and there was the letter for Orin Porter Rockwell. The return address was in Jefferson City, and it was from Uzziah O'Bannon. Boy, did she want to open that letter, but it was Porter's and she respected his privacy. Maybe she would take him a hot lunch today at the quarry, and just happen to bring the letter along.

3

The days after the letter to Porter rolled by just like the others had, Uzziah imagined. He slept in his little house and dreamed of Hannah and the baby, and when he wasn't doing that, he was thinking about the blessing which Orin Porter Rockwell had given him right before he left Nauvoo. Now, Uzziah was a superstitious man, and it came with the territory when you were from Virginia. His ma, Rahab, had all kinds of sayings, and he'd taken each one to heart, sure that his other brothers and sisters had done the same.

The blessing? What did it really mean? He didn't think it meant much till he was standing in the saloon and the Jefferson Penitentiary guard was unloading on him, and he hadn't been hit. Granted, he was hoping he'd be killed so he could join Hannah, and that wasn't right, that was as good as suicide, and he knew it. God did not like his creation calling it quits until God said it was time to come home. So, the blessing? There was only one way to figure it out, and that was to go about as if the blessing was true, that neither gun nor knife could touch him as long as he kept his hair long. Well, that wouldn't be hard. Ever since he'd gone to the mountains, he'd let it grow, and it was plenty long now.

The hearing for Pete Betz was coming up at the courthouse, and, of course, Uzziah would have to attend. He was the peace officer who had been drawn on, and if he didn't show up, well, the warrant would be vacated. The day of the court hearing, he was down at Buck's having breakfast. Well, he liked the company, and Buck and Beth both appreciated it. They had tried to have children, and truthfully, Uzziah was old enough to be theirs, and Beth secretly harbored in her heart that he could be, if she wished it hard enough. She had started reading the Bible more since Uzziah showed up, and when a grown man has an influence like that on older people, that can be nothing but good.

He was sitting having the last of a huge breakfast, which he was sure Beth wouldn't have fixed if he hadn't come down like he was beginning to always do.

"Court today," Buck said, and it wasn't neutral the way he said it.

"Should be open and shut, right? I appear, they swear me in, and I testify to the fact that Peter Betz threw down on me, and away he goes to the Jefferson City penitentiary."

Buck looked at Uzziah, then at Beth, and he made up his mind, "Beth, can ya get me that scarf I likes to wear when the weather's damp, please?"

"Sure, hon," she said and left the kitchen.

Buck had purposely hidden the scarf so it'd take her longer to find than usual.

"Listen, Uzziah, you ain't the first to try and testify against Gongloe's men."

"Oh yeah," Uzziah said, shoveling in the last of the huckleberry pancakes Beth had made.

"No, no, there's surely been others, but the two that's tried, they's up on boot hill."

"So," Uzziah started in, and Beth showed up with Buck's scarf.

"Here ya go, hon."

"That ain't my favorite."

"Sure, it's always been yer favorite."

"Used to be, now, I likes the robin's egg blue one," he said and handed her back his favorite scarf.

She harrumphed and left the kitchen and mumbled something on the way to the bedroom.

"Gongloe's men kilt 'em?" Uzziah asked excited, it seemed it was time to test his blessing, and it wouldn't be arbitrary, that is, he wouldn't go looking for a fight, the fight would come to him.

"Yeah, son, they did. Ifn ya don't want to go, hell, I'd understand," Buck said and smiled before he swallowed the last of his coffee. "Let's get goin', we're gonna be late."

Beth came into the kitchen with the robin's egg blue scarf and was holding it out to Buck while he was at the back door, "Yer scarf!"

"Nah, don't need it today, ain't that damp," Buck said, and as he closed the door, he thought he heard a string of oaths against him.

They rode to the sheriff's office, and as per usual, Willy had the coffee going and Pete was yelling something to him from the cells in the back. Both men walked in, and Uzziah had taken a fairly good look at the street and those who were on it early this morning. Didn't look any different than any other time since he'd arrived in town.

"What's he hollerin' 'bout?" Buck asked Willy.

"Somethin' 'bout being set free today 'cause there would be no one to testify agin' him," Willy said and hoped Uzziah hadn't heard.

"Oh, I'll testify all right, ya can count on that," Uzziah said.

"I wish ya wouldn't. I like Frank a lot and he wanted to set things straight in Jeff City, but maybe they's okay the way they is," Willy said hopefully.

"Nah, they ain't, me and Uzziah's gonna ride to the courthouse together, and ifn there's trouble, they'll be two guns to deal with the varmints," Buck said, raising his cup of coffee in a toast.

"I'm goin' alone, Buck, understand?"

"Alone?"

"Yeah, as in by myself."

"But—"

"No buts, just me walkin' to the courthouse."

"Ya ain't even gonna ride that fast hoss of yern?"

"Nope, it's not a bad day, and by lunchtime, it'll be a fine walk."

"Well, at least y'all have Pete with ya, maybe ya can use him as a shield and Gongloe's men can do the whole town a favor," Buck said and chuckled, but Uzziah knew he was telling him how to take the prisoner in, and the part about the shield, well, why not?

Buck and Uzziah made their rounds that morning, checking in with the businesses up and down the strip and even some of the side streets. There was a Chinese section of town, where Gongloe had himself a mansion built. It had the tips of the roofs pointing skyward like some Chinese temple, and all the doors inside slid on railings instead of being like regular people's doors. At the very top, there was a widow's walk, a big one. The whole place was painted a bright yellow, and Uzziah thought about something.

"Hey, let's go by and see how the Chinese community are doin'?"

"What!?"

"Let's check on some constituents that get ignored, what ya say?" Uzziah was all happy and turned Shadow down 5th Street and up into the Chinese community. It was like any other community, it was morning, and they were all starting their day.

"This is kinda off limits to the sheriff," Buck said.

"It shouldn't be, after all, these people live within the city limits and should be afforded the same protection," Uzziah said, and just as he finished saying that, a rather large man, who was Chinese, was hauling a little Chinaman from his laundry by the scruff of his neck and the two of them were in a Chinese shouting match. Uzziah thought it sounded like dogs trying to talk.

He rode Shadow over and knocked the horse into the bigger Chinaman, and he had to let go of his victim to keep himself from falling over.

Immediately, he pulled a curved blade from his belt

and flung it at Uzziah, who simply held up the Hawken, and the blade twanged home in the stock.

Sheriff Laurie took in a great breath, and Uzziah simply pulled the knife from the stock of the Hawken and placed it in his saddlebags.

"That mine!" the big Chinaman yelled.

"Not anymore it ain't," Uzziah said. "I believe ya just gave it to me, ifn ya want it back come to the sheriff's office."

Uzziah got off Shadow and ground tied him, then walked over to where the little man was trying to adjust his shirt, coat, and tie.

"Ya okay?" Uzziah said louder than usual, thinking that if the guy didn't speak English, maybe speaking louder would assist in his understanding.

"Why you yell, I no deaf," the man objected. "Nothing but private matter, you go, leave alone," he added.

Uzziah looked at the bigger Chinaman, who was smiling as in an *I told you so*, kind of smirk.

It was then that Gongloe stepped from his mansion with several western bodyguards, they were heavily armed.

"What do we owe this visit?" he asked cordially.

"Just thought ya'd wanna see me afore ya tried to kill me," Uzziah said boldly.

"Whatever do you mean?" Gongloe asked, smiling.

"Ya know what I mean, and I will see ya in court, ifn yer gonna be there, and the prisoner Peter Betts will be with me."

"Are you sure?" Gongloe asked as he stepped onto the steps leading into the stylish carriage, which was purported to have bulletproof glass in the windows, at least that's what Buck had told him.

"Sure as rain," Uzziah said, and the rain started, and Gongloe looked up with a quizzical expression.

They followed the fancy carriage all the way to the Golden Owl—well, Uzziah followed the carriage, and Sheriff Buck Laurie followed Uzziah, looking left and right at every alleyway.

"I ain't never seen nothin' like yer gumption, Uzziah," Buck said and spat into the road.

"What kinda gumption does this take?"

"Nah, not this, this is just fullering. The way ya almost knocked down the big Chinamen."

"What's goin' on with that?" Uzziah asked, and Buck rode up alongside Uzziah so he could speak softly.

"All the Chinese businesses pay him to protect 'em," Buck said, smirking.

"And if they don't pay?"

"Then someone roughs 'em up or their businesses get set on fire," Buck said, "It's disgraceful, mostly 'cause he's a treatin' his own people thataway."

When they got to the main street and the Golden Owl, Uzziah and Buck peeled off, and when Gongloe got out, he looked over his shoulder at them.

"That man is scary," Buck said.

"No, that man is scared," Uzziah said, knowing it was probably the first time since Gongloe had started in business in Jefferson City that anybody had stood up to him who wasn't shortly dead.

Back at the sheriff's office, Beth had brought a light

lunch for the men, and Willy was already eating his sandwich when the two co-sheriffs walked in.

"Did ya bless that food?" Uzziah asked Willy, who almost choked on the bite he'd taken.

"I blessed it fer 'em afore I brought it over," Beth said, and it seemed to everyone there that she had come to say her unofficial goodbyes to Uzziah, since she didn't expect him to live through the afternoon.

He wasn't hungry, but he didn't want to disappoint Bethany, so he ate two of the three sandwiches she'd fixed him, promising to finish the other when he got back from the courthouse.

As he was leaving, on foot, as he said he was going to do, and pushing the handcuffed prisoner in front of him, she stepped out and waved and yelled, "Goodbye!"

"See ya soon!" he yelled back, but didn't look back toward her. There was no telling when the attack of attacks would take place.

It was a twenty-minute walk to the courthouse, and Pete Betz had crowed the first fifteen minutes of it, but the closer they got to his judgment, the less he spoke, until he had his head on a swivel and sure hoped whoever was gunning would not accidentally shoot him!

Finally, on turning the corner at Gaston and Main, the Jefferson County Courthouse was up ahead. Betz lost it.

"Just let me go, ifn they sees ya let me go, they'll let ya live, just lct mc go!" he pleaded.

"No, sir, we're walkin' in there and yer gonna be charged with what ya done, and then you'll serve yer time," Uzziah said.

He noticed a lot of people around the courthouse, coming and going. There were carriages and freight wagons, horses, and well, throngs of people, he said a silent prayer that all bullets or other means of death which missed him might also miss the innocent.

As he climbed the stairs, someone shouted, "Now!"

Several of those whom Uzziah had thought were just folks on the street were actually Gongloe's men—he counted six of them, four with pistols, one with a rifle, and one had a Greener, which he was bringing up from under a long drover's coat. That would take a couple seconds, so he concentrated on the others. He lifted the Hawken he always carried and fired up to the second story of the courthouse, where a man was leaning out the window with a Winchester.

The man screamed as he fired. The shot ricocheted off the steps beside Uzziah, and he couldn't tell where it went. The body of the rifleman hung from the window at his waist and blood was flowing down the side of the courthouse.

In the meantime, the Greener was lifted, and the man was standing in the middle of a crowd with some children. A tomahawk flew through the air with deadly accuracy, and the man stood there with his brachial artery severed and blood pumping into the sleeve of his drover's coat and running out at the sleeve of that arm. The Greener hit the ground, went off, and took out the legs of one of the pistoleros, who went down screaming and not thinking about shooting anybody.

The three other pistoleros kept firing and ricochet after ricochet careened off the steps of the courthouse, as Uzziah pulled his pistol and, aiming well as lead flew past him, shot them dead on the spot, center mass shots which stopped their hearts.

Pete Betz was frozen in place. Luckily, he had been standing just close enough to Uzziah that the blessing must have covered him, too. He kept feeling around on his body as if he would find a wound, any wound. His countenance after that was like a small child as he looked to Uzziah to be told what to do.

The courthouse guards were out on the steps, their weapons drawn, but the action was ended. Children were screaming and pointing at a man who had exsanguinated through the sleeve of his drover's coat, women had them held close and were trying to console them.

"Get that man hanging from the window," one of the guards yelled to someone who ran inside the courthouse. The other guards surrounded Uzziah and a meek, little man who seemed to be cowering next to him and they led them into the courthouse.

Beth, Buck, and Willy had retired to the picnic table behind the jailhouse. When Buck had first started the job before Mr. Gongloe had arrived in Jeff City, she had made a flower garden back there with perennials. They were all dead now because of the temperature, but on nice days like this, the sheriff, his wife, and his deputy like to sit back there and look up at the bluing sky, and watch the scudding clouds race by.

They had been back there when the shooting at the courthouse was going on, and Beth had spilled her coffee and then started crying as soon as the shooting was over. Willy wondered if maybe he should be the proper deputy and not the boy who swept up, opened up the jail, and went to the café to get prisoners' meals, but then he didn't like the notion of being riddled with bullets any more than the next man.

Buck comforted Bethany as best he could. He had his arm around her, and her sobs had turned to hiccups, which usually meant the crying was over, or at least that was his personal experience.

When they heard the footsteps on the gravel path that led to the garden, they cowered for just a moment. Well, Buck did draw his revolver, but if it was Gongloe and his men, he'd use it on Beth to keep her from being tortured and raped.

"Hey, y'all," Uzziah said in a cheerful voice, and the three people back there didn't know what to say. "Heck, I didn't even know this was back cheer, ya knows I gots me a green thumb, yes I do—" He was going to say more, but Bethany had run into his arms, crying again.

Oh, great, through Buck, *I'll have to comfort her again*. But these were tears of absolute and unbelievable joy.

Daniel had survived the lions' den. Meshack, Shadrack, and Abednego had made it through the fire, and like that story, there was another with them in the fire, and that was who was standing by Uzziah, well, at least that's what he thought the blessing meant, so why not?

Willy let off a whistle and a cowboy holler. "Yee Haw!" he screamed at the top of his voice, and Buck kept looking for leaking wounds on his new co-sheriff.

There were the usual *what happened* questions, and as best he could, he went through the events of the courthouse steps, play by play, and Willy dreamed that he had been there, and assisted, and well, so did Buck. But they hadn't, they had held back thinking that the little house would have to be cleaned up of Uzziah's stuff, and the next deputy, maybe a wiser and more prudent man, would take his place, and come over for breakfasts, but who, who could take the place of Uzziah!?!

That night, as Uzziah kneeled by the bed in the little bedchamber, he folded his hands together and burst into tears. Once again, he had supposed that the blessing from Porter Rockwell had been just words over a friend's carcass, and he had gone into the event as if he would be with Hannah in their celestial marriage, and he wondered to himself, *What would that look like?* Did they all—these celestial brides and grooms—have houses, in a row on a hill, or were they fairly much as they had been in a celestial Nauvoo and the little cabin would now be the immutable little cabin, and the light outside the simple glory of the one and only God?

No night, no war, no death, no hunger. Well, he did remember that Jesus had barbequed fish for the disciples on the shore of the Sea of Galilee, and Peter had jumped whip when he recognized Jesus and swam to shore. It says right there in the gospel, Jesus ate with the disciples that morning, and for a big man like Uzziah, he clung to that delicious fact!

He asked for forgiveness in thinking that the blessing by Porter had been nothing but nice words said over a departing friend, and he began to think what it would be like to go through the rest of his life without harm from blade or bullet. It had said nothing about claw, tooth, or just being squeezed to death by a griz, or falling off a high place. Then he started thinking about Jesus's baptism, and how he had been led into the desert where he was tempted by the Prince of the Power of the Air, the king of liars. He was hungry and Satan told him to change the rocks to bread, he was humbled and Satan offered him the kingdoms of this earth, if he would only bow down, he was taken to a high place, and told to jump because surely the angels would protect him as it said in the Psalms, not letting his foot be struck against a stone!?!

He felt as if he might go crazy holding this knowledge by himself, and he was waiting anxiously for Porter to get here, for Porter to explain what the blessing meant, and how it was to be used, and where, and all the questions—my God!

He fell asleep kneeling at the side of the bed, and when he wakened, he realized that his prayers had been all about him, he hadn't talked to Hannah, although there were those who said the dead were beyond being talked to, but hadn't the rich man in hell seen the beggar at his gate, who was now in heaven and hadn't he asked him for a drop of water, just a drop!?! Didn't they talk, and weren't they both dead?

He talked to Hannah because he had to. He asked her what the blessing could mean, or was it a curse? He asked her what he should do with the troubles in Jefferson City, but hadn't she already told him? Hadn't she mouthed the words from Galatians, hadn't he seen her in his mind's eye and read her lips, wasn't that why he had taken the job and now was possibly endangering the sheriff, Bethany, and the boy, Willy? He would never forgive himself if all this—it could only be pride, all this pride led to their deaths! That would be the ultimate end of his pride, and if that happened, what then?

When he awakened in the morning, he felt better, not great, but better. He would tell Buck, Beth, and Willy about the blessing, and they could advise him, or think him crazy. He sure wished Orin Porter Rockwell would arrive in town.

Uzziah had no way of knowing what was happening that morning—the morning after the courthouse shootings, as it was being called. He had no way of knowing that Buck and Beth had prayed about Uzziah, and who he was, and if he was one of those strangers you entertained and they turned out to be angels.

They were confused, and Willy had come over for breakfast, because the confusion in all the town was growing into some sort of critical mass. Even Mr. Gongloe had called a meeting of all his lieutenants and was asking all of them, "Who the hell is this guy!?! Can't anybody kill him!!"

So, when Uzziah rode up on Shadow, there was a hint of what it would have been like for people to feed the Messiah. It wasn't that he was the Christ, they all knew that, but he was somebody, all right! Somebody who wasn't like other folks. He didn't seem to have a shred of fear in him, and when things happened around him, his heart must have slowed, and his reactions became the reactions of a man who knew he was destined to win, a man—like the Christ—who had given it all up to the father in the—was it vain glory!?!? To think that after death on the cross, after being smothered by his own weight, after facing death with your mother, and your brothers standing by, and being naked and hanging up there like a common criminal, was it vain glory to imagine the day in three days when—?

They could hear Uzziah putting Shadow in the barn with Buck's roan, and then his steps long and even as he made it to the front door, they tried to act natural, but when the door opened and he was coming through it, something in all three of them zinged and they were uplifted!

It got easier to be around Uzziah after that. The criminal element in Jeff City slowed way down, as if they, too, were reeling from the impossible being possible, and the days dragged on and nothing particularly different happened. Men who were confronted with Uzziah, and the whole sheriff's staff, actually, men confronted by them, just went along knowing it was useless to act against what—a force which threatened to break human bondage!?!

4

Uzziah hadn't forgotten about the letter which he'd sent Porter Rockwell, but it had slipped his mind how many days it had been since. He was getting ready to have breakfast with Beth and Buck when he heard hoofbeats outside his little house that was on the Missouri. He got his pistol out and had it behind his back when he opened the front door and stood off to the side. The light wasn't great from the east as yet, and it was cloudy, but there was no mistaking Porter's limp when he got off his horse and gimped toward the front door.

"How'd ya know where I lived?"

"Got in last night, stayed at that place they call a hotel, weren't too bad, but it was late, didn't want to bother ya," he said as the two men embraced.

"Still, how'd ya know?"

"Are ya kiddin' me! Everyone, I do mean everyone, in town knows where the great Uzziah O'Bannon lives," Porter said, then added, "Ya got any whiskey?"

"Yeah," Uzziah said, remembering fonder days with

his partner in the mountains, as he went into the kitchen and brought out a bottle of Jameson.

Porter just stood there with the bottle in his hand.

"I can't believe this!" he said, looking at the bottle.

"Well, there's been a lot of that recently," Uzziah said.

"Oh yeah," Porter said as he uncorked the bottle, and asked, "Glasses?"

Uzziah just motioned with his hand and Porter tipped it up and brought it back down again.

"So, from yer letter, well, it was really just a *help note,* I get the idea ya could use a hand with a Chinaman?"

"Yeah, more of that later today," Uzziah said, sitting at the table in the parlor. "I need to know about that blessing ya gave me?"

"Ain't worked, ya got stabbed and shot!" Porter joked as he took a seat at the same table, and the two men laughed.

"No, quite the opposite. I've gone up against some incredible odds and was unscathed," Uzziah said and turned his head a bit.

"Yep, that's the way it works, same thing can be said fer me. So, how many of these Chinamen ya got to deal with?"

"It's only the boss who's Chinese, some of his crew are, but only in little Chinatown," Uzziah said, then he went on and told Porter about the courthouse steps and the shootout there, and his not getting a scratch.

"What can I tell ya, the blessing which I passed on from the prophet, obviously workin' fer ya. Ya should be glad, no?"

"I am, but this lull in the action worries me," Uzziah said.

"Yeah, tell ya what worries me, is everybody knowing where yer house sits, by the way, nice place," Porter said.

"Thanks, this place belongs to Sheriff Laurie, Buck Laurie, he's a great guy, but getting up there in years, and he and his wife live just about a rifle shot from here."

"That ain't good," Porter said, taking another sip.

"Why not? I eat with 'em every morning."

"Routine like that gonna git all y'all kilt, Uzziah. Ya can't be doin' things on some schedule, soon as it's learned they earned the right to shoot ya down. Ifn yer eating breakfast with the sheriff and his wife every workday morning, they probably already got a plan to hit the sheriff's place!"

"Ya think they'd be that bold?"

"They had things goin' their way till ya showed up, and the sooner they get rid of ya and the man who hired ya, well, that sends a message, don't it?"

"Well, let's go over and tell the sheriff all about it."

"No, ya got a café ya like?"

"Yeah, on 2nd Street, real good food," Uzziah said.

"Well, they don't knows me, so this morning, I'm gonna go tell the sheriff and his wife to join us there, do they know the place?"

"Yeah, we go there for supper sometimes."

"Good, go a different route into town, ifn ya know one, I'll let the sheriff in, just hope he ain't layin' over there with his throat cut," Porter said.

"Ya think it's that bad?"

"Uzziah, we Latter-Day Saints been dealin' with

this shite fer a long time, it only gets worse, why do ya think the prophet blessed me like he did? It ain't fer me, it's fer him! Now, that reminds me. I got a week, one week to wind this up chere, then I gots to get back and protect Joe, okay?"

"Yeah, sure, see ya at the café," Uzziah said and slipped out the back way and went into the barn by the man door and saddled up Shadow. They had all been fed, and Jenny, thankfully, didn't bray.

Uzziah rode past the sheriff's house, looking at it briefly as he rode by at a gallop, then went into town the back way.

Porter had taken his now pregnant mare, the one who had frolicked with Shadow when the two men had just met, and waited until Uzziah was totally out of sight. Then, he walked her down to the river and over in front of the sheriff's house. Then, tying her up to a tree by the Missouri, he snuck up to the sheriff's house. As he was making his way to the back of the house, he saw two men sneaking in the bushes off to the west. He stayed real still and made sure it was only two. It was, he cocked his Navy Colts, he'd brought an extra one, and taking the sawed-off shotgun from under his coat, he ran up on the house from the east, keeping the house between himself and the two men sneaking in.

He opened a window on that side of the house, and could hear a man and a woman's voice in the kitchen. He walked from the bedroom where he entered the house to the kitchen doorway and put his index finger to his lips.

The first one to see him was thankfully the sheriff, women do have a tendency to scream, and the sheriff went over to his wife like he was going to kiss her, and he twisted her around and put his hand over her mouth, she struggled not understanding what was happening until she saw the motionless figure in the kitchen doorway.

"Uzziah sent me. I'm Porter Rockwell. There are two men sneaking up on this house from the west."

The sheriff whispered something to his wife, and she pulled up a trap door and went into the root cellar, so they were safe for the time being.

"Whatcha want me to do?" Buck asked Porter before he closed the trapdoor.

"Get down there with yer wife, sir," he said respectively.

Sheriff Laurie looked at Porter strangely, then did just what the man said and climbed down into the root cellar.

In the root cellar, it was dark except for a bit of light that shot through the space between the floorboards in the kitchen. They heard a bunch of scurrying around, and then Porter was in and out of the kitchen, then the most amazing thing happened. He started talking to himself, but he disguised his voice in answer as a woman's voice. It was a very good imitation. It didn't sound like Beth or Buck, but it did sound like two different people. Then they heard the pantry door open and close, and then he continued for a bit with the faking of the voices, then silence.

They could hear the soft footsteps of someone coming from the westside of the house, through the parlor into the kitchen, then a blasting of guns which lasted maybe five seconds, as it seemed a lot of bullets were fired, then one of the men said, "What the hell!" and they heard the pantry doors open slowly and there were two shotgun blasts and the sound of bodies falling —two of them.

Uzziah was a bit surprised by how long it took Buck, Beth, and Porter to get to the café, but he ordered coffee, then a refill, then a muffin, then he got worried.

Then, smiling and laughing, two women came walking through the door of the café with Porter. What the hell!

When they sat down, both women faced toward the wall where Uzziah had gotten a table. Beth was one of them, but the other one was Sheriff Laurie in a dress and wearing a veil!

"What the hell happened?"

It was a simple question, but Beth and Buck started talking at the same time, and Porter just sat back and poured a little whiskey into his coffee from a flask Uzziah had never seen—maybe it was his traveling flask.

The gist of the story Uzziah got. Buck and Beth had been hidden in the root cellar below the kitchen. Porter had made dummies out of the pillows and thrown clothes over them, then put out the lamp. The pistoleros came in, shot the pillows up, then when they lit a match, discovered they had murdered bedclothes, then

Porter quietly opened the pantry and blew them into the parlor with his sawed-off shotgun.

"What'd ya do with the bodies?"

"Yer gonna like this part," Buck said.

"I dressed them up in Buck and Beth's clothes, took them to the mortician, and dumped them into coffins, and told 'im they was so bad shot-up that there'd be no open coffin stuff, then nailed 'em shut," Porter said.

"He was a good friend of ours, pretty torn up, Porter said." Buck was smiling when he told the story.

"Funeral will be the day after tommarie," added Beth.

"They's gonna go to Beth's sister's in the country, far from here."

"We're picking up Willy on the way," Buck added.

"Better git goin' afore the word of yer demise gets out," Porter said, and he and Uzziah walked the two *ladies* out to the carriage, and they took off for the jail.

Porter and Uzziah mounted up and followed them. They got Willy, who seemed confused, but went along with it. They rode out to the city limits and saw the carriage disappear into the morning fog.

"I'm hungry," Uzziah said.

"Back to the café," was all Porter said and clicked up his pregnant mare.

They had asked the waitress to hold the back table for them. They sat and ordered grits, eggs over medium, sausage patties and ham steaks, and lots of biscuits. As they ate, plans were made.

"In a few hours, the whole of Jeff City will know

Sheriff Laurie and his wife are dead, what do we do?" Uzziah asked.

"Well, when the little cotton tails are snuggled in their warm dens beneath the earth, do ya think they give any mind to the coyotes who are above 'em all hungry and waitin' fer them to come out at night, huh? How 'bout them owls and hawks which sit up during the day surveying their kingdoms, and thinkin' 'bout the little bunnies comin' out and feedin' their young, what 'bout them?"

Uzziah looked at Porter oddly, then asked, "Is this line of reasonin' goin' somewhere or are ya just being a nature lover or somethin'?"

"Listen, we done sent the bunnies off to their dens, didn't we? I mean, the good old sheriff and his pretty little wife are safe. The hawks and coyotes of this world can't touch 'em now, so there's only one thing left to do, young son,"

"And that would be?" Uzziah asked, thinking maybe Porter had dipped into his flask a bit hard this morning.

"Cut off the head of the snake!" Porter said, and as they finished their plates, Uzziah knew why Porter was a gunman, not a poet. His mixture of metaphors would have made Immanuel smile.

It was still early when the two men rode into little Chinatown. The mansion was shrouded in the fog, which had gotten worse since sunup. Eventually, it would roll back to the Missouri, where it would evaporate, but now it gave a ghostly appearance to everything.

"Ya got what we're gonna do?" Porter asked Uzziah.

"Yeah, ya got enough ammunition on ya?"

"Always, and don't fergit the prophet's blessing on both of us, I passed it onto ya. No blade or bullet will touch us, I'm just hoping there ain't a tiger in the Chinaman's house," Porter added and chuckled.

Uzziah was amazed. How could the man joke at a time like this? Yes, it had seemed since he'd received the blessing and laying on of hands from Porter, that he was safe from blade or bullet, but still, they were walking right into the lion's den.

They tied their horses up behind the old chain-men's laundry. He was out back smoking a pipe. When Porter smelled it, he walked over to the old man.

He said something in Chinese to him, and Uzziah's jaw hit the ground. The old man loaded the pipe again and handed it to Porter. He lit it up, took a big puff, and held in the smoke, then handed it to Uzziah.

"Opium. Will slow things down fer us, we'll see everythin' like it was happening in slow motion," he said while holding his breath.

What the hell, they were walking into hell, and Porter seemed to have an idea how to do just that. Uzziah took a big puff, held it, and passed the pipe to Porter, who took another, and passed the pipe back. Uzziah waved the pipe off. He could already feel things slowing down. Porter handed the pipe back to the old Chinaman with a rather large denomination of a bill wrapped around it. The Chinaman bowed, and so did Porter.

"How ya know chink speak?"

"The gospel of the Latter-Day Saints is goin' every-where, plus there was a Chinese laundry down the street from where I was brought up, and I liked their singsong words, so I learned some."

Uzziah was thinking about Porter Rockwell learning Chinese when Porter tapped him on the shoulder.

"Come on, cuss, this one's fer Hannah," Porter said.

Uzziah was confused. Why would this one be for Hannah? But when he stopped thinking about that, they were walking up the gravel path to Gongloe's mansion. Right up to the front door! Uzziah thought he saw a curtain open on the top floor where he imagined the chief Chinaman slept. When he looked up, the curtain closed. Well, good, he guessed, they knew they were coming, but short of a Bengal tiger, what had they to fear? Then Uzziah remembered a scripture, Psalm 118, the 6th verse, and he said it out loud for Porter to hear. "*The Lord is on my side, I will not be afraid. What can man do to me?*"

"That's the spirit, young son," Porter said as bullets flew through the front door of the mansion without it even being opened. Uzziah could hear them sizzling past them like angry bees.

Porter unloaded the sawed-off shotgun through the doors, and two chainmen came stumbling out and fell down the steps dead.

"You take the downstairs, I'm going for the head of the snake," Uzziah said as he walked up the long spiral staircase. He could hear shots being fired behind him and men yelling out in their deaths.

Someone came running down the stairs, firing two pistols, but nothing touched Uzziah. He gutted the man with his Bowie as he ran past him, and he fell trying to hold his intestines in, tumbling down the stairs, getting entangled in the bloody things.

At the top of the stairs, two Anglo cowboys were firing wildly at Uzziah, but he shot both of them in the stomachs and they were soon rolling past him on the staircase. The stairs opened to a big room which was empty, then it led down a narrow hallway to the end, where he saw Gongloe slamming and locking the door.

"Kill him! Kill him!" he shouted to his minions, and his accent seemed to worsen when he was stressed. Now he sounded like the old man at the laundry, not the sophisticated operator of saloons, whorehouses, and rackets.

The first door he came to, Uzziah shot through it without looking. A man came out, shot through the chest. Then three doors opened, the last had a man with a shotgun. Uzziah grabbed the first man out, knocked his pistol away with the Hawken, and held him like a shield in front of him. He could feel the man's insides splattered up against his good Mormon clothes. He tomahawked the man with the shotgun in the back as he ran down the hall, reaching for whatever it was that was stuck in his back.

A Chinaman stepped from the last door before Gongloe's and threw tiny, sharp objects at Uzziah. He held up the Hawken, and all four of them implanted themselves in the stock. The next man out of a door was raked from his belly to his chin with the four death stars that protruded from the stock of the Hawken, then Uzziah scraped them off the stock by using the doorpost that the man had come out of.

He turned and looked down the hall just in time to see a man rolling a small cannon into the large room and aiming it down the hall. The man touched fire to the fuse and Uzziah hit the floor as the cannon exploded, the twelve-pound ball shimmied over his inert body and slammed into the reinforced door behind which Gongloe was hiding. The door was splintered as Uzziah rolled over and fired the Hawken down the hall at the man who was running at him with what looked like a meat cleaver. The man was shot through and through and ran right over Uzziah and into the room where Gongloe was hiding, and was welcomed by two shotgun blasts which threw him out an upstairs window, the glass shattering, and into the garden below.

The shooting from downstairs had stopped, and Porter was yelling as he walked up the staircase. "It's me, don't shoot," he said in a singsong voice, which amused Uzziah. It was then that he realized he felt wonderful. Nothing that had happened had rattled him, and the glow which he felt in his body must surely be from the opium. Well, he had wondered what that might feel like, and now he knew.

They both walked up the spiral wrought-iron stairs that led to the widow's walk above. Gongloe was doing something up there, and the sounds were not familiar to them. Fearing some bizarre Chinese weapon, they hesitated long enough, then they saw through the broken window, which one of his guards had crashed through, a very large bird fly off.

"What in the name of heaven was that!?!" Porter yelled.

"That was him!" Uzziah shouted as they both scrambled up the spiral stairs and out onto the widow's walk.

They stood out there and watched as Gongloe was

literally flying through the air toward the Missouri River. As it turned out, the Chinese had developed the first hang gliders as untethered kites and forced prisoners to jump off cliffs tied to them. Great amusement for the emperor. Unfortunately, for the emperor, when Gongloe had been tied to one such devise, he flew over two miles, and always remembered the design of the devise which had saved his life.

"I think he's going to the river," Porter said. "Does he have a boat?"

"You go, the fog is lifting," Uzziah said, strangely unaffected by the master criminal's escape.

"I'll see ya back at the café," Porter yelled as he ran for the main staircase. Uzziah heard several shots—some of the wounded must have roused themselves only to be shot down by Porter.

Fascinated, Uzziah watched as Gongloe flew closer and closer to the river. Several times, he raised his Hawken, but the flight was erratic in the rising fog, and Uzziah simply laid on the widow's walk and waited. Soon, Gongloe disappeared as he lowered the winged devise into the thickest part of the morning fog.

He stretched out there on the widow's walk and thought for a moment that he smelled smoke, but it was early morning, and all of Jefferson City would be starting up wood or coal fires, so he dismissed the smell. He aimed his Hawken down from where he thought Gongloe had landed along the river, and waited.

Then, God sent the wind, that was the way Uzziah could think about it. Father, as in his Heavenly Father, had sent a wind to foil the Chinaman, and it did. The fog lifted and rose up away from the river, and then Uzziah saw the boat. It was powered by steam and had a small, but seemed efficient, side paddle. It was steaming Gongloe and the men on it, those sailors who must have been kept in ready just in case, down the Missouri toward Saint Louis.

When the fog lifted, the side paddle was a good 300 yards away and going nicely with the current. It wouldn't be that difficult a shot. He lined it up and squeezed the trigger, and the hammer fell on an unloaded gun! So much for the benefits of opium!

He grabbed his powder horn and everything else and started loading. It seemed like it took forever, again an aftereffect of the opiate. When he lined the shot up again, the steamer had gone quite a ways further. The side paddle was at least 1000 yards away and moving steadily downstream.

He raised the rifle, sighted with the open blade sight on the head of Gongloe, then raised the rifle just enough for the 54-caliber shot to hit its target, and squeezed. He had time to lower the rifle and wait, then a wonderful blood-red spray appeared momentarily over Gongloe's head and his body dropped to the floor of the pilot house.

The same wind that had lifted the fog had also wafted the flames that had started in Gongloe's mansion. At some point in the firefight, a lamp had been knocked over or exploded.

Orin Porter Rockwell had been galloping his pregnant mare down the bank of the Missouri and had just caught sight of the side paddle and the man they were after standing in the pilot house, when a crimson blossom bloomed above that head and the man had dropped dead. Damn! Uzziah had done that!

When Porter turned, he saw way back from where he was that there was a big house fire, and he remembered the exploding oil lamp which he'd shot through to kill a guard, then he spurred his mare back toward the mansion.

When he got there, the entire Chinese community was gathered around and watching the blaze, but it wasn't exactly the blaze they were watching. They were morbidly curious about the rather large man who stood on the widow's walk of the house and was holding a long rifle.

Porter tied the mare up to a tree a couple of blocks from the fire. Horses hate fires and will do anything to avoid them. In deference to his mare, he tied a rag around her head so that she could not see the flames. They hate fires, but they cannot stop watching them when they appear.

He ran the two blocks back into little Chinatown and got as close to the fire as he could. The heat was tremendous.

"Uzziah! Uzziah!" he screamed up at the man.

Uzziah came over to that side of the widow's walk. Fortunately, it was an open structure, and it was longer than it was wide. It was essentially the third story of this mansion, and even the basement had height, so it was well off the ground. He looked down, and there stood Porter. Yes, he was safe from blade or bullet, but the prophet had not mentioned anything about fire. Uzziah guessed that would have meant that he would be immune, perhaps to the flames of hell, then?

"Jump! Jump!" Porter kept urging, and he was

pointing to a rather large—at least 75-foot Ohio buckeye. The limbs were sparse down toward the ground, but up at Uzziah's level, there were plenty.

"Jump to the big tree!" Porter was now yelling.

Uzziah considered several things just as he would when making a long-distance shot. The wind, well, it was minimal, too bad it wasn't blowing a gale toward that big buckeye. The distance from the end of the widow's walk to the tree, which he judged to be about fifty feet. Far enough away not to be bothered by the flames of the mansion now going up in flames, but perhaps too far for his 275 pounds of body weight to make it.

Foolishly, he looked around for another one of those winged things Gongloe had escaped with. There had been only one. Then, he heard the sound of something collapsing, and the house began to tilt toward the tree. Well, that was one thing. He threw everything he could down toward Porter, the Hawken, his powder horn, and anything else that might hinder him. He would stay dressed, if he fell to his death, at least he'd be clothed, and not quite the ultimate spectacle of a big naked man falling to his death. Plus, he'd need the clothes to buffer his body when, and if, he made it that far.

Hitting that tree was going to scuff him up a bit! The mansion tilted once again, and now the widow's walk was a runway downhill pointing to the big buckeye. Uzziah took off running as fast as he had ever run in his life, hoping to jump at the very last to give himself an extra advantage. As he ran, he wondered how many bones he'd break when he missed the tree.

Time was still slowed by the opiate, and when he jumped up to come down on the edge of the widow's walk and make his jump, the widow's walk fell away, and he was sliding down with the debris from it toward he knew now what. He closed his eyes, and all of a sudden, he was soaking wet, and when he looked up, hellfire was raining down on him.

There are times in a man's life when he sees, actually sees God's grace in action. Porter had encouraged his new best friend to jump to the stately tree, and when Uzziah had tried to launch himself off the corner of the widow's walk, it collapsed. But then Porter saw God's plan, not his.

God had planned for Uzziah to ride the broken trash of the widow's walk down into the awaiting duckpond, which everyone in little Chinatown admired greatly, thinking that it was possibly one of the best features of the mansion. It would have killed Uzziah to jump down into it, but coming down as he did on the slide provided by the broken widow's walk, he was swept into it, and when he surfaced, the flaming remains of that part of the mansion rained down on him. Well, maybe that wasn't part of God's plan.

Uzziah surfaced on the other side of the duckpond, wet but unscathed, and the people of little Chinatown cheered in their Chinese way as he was pulled out the pond by Porter Rockwell.

Jefferson City had been under a cloud of crime that they had only half suspected. When the crime boss was done away with, Porter had been right, cut off the head of the snake, and those who worked for him scattered to the four winds.

Back in the little house just off the Missouri River, Uzziah was recovering from the fall he'd taken. Really, outwardly, there was nothing wrong with him, but inwardly, he thought he was about to die, and even if it meant being with Hannah Larue and his infant son, well, he still wasn't happy about it.

"When are ya leavin'?" he asked Porter, who had been gathering his things together. He had stayed with Uzziah for three days since the burning down of the mansion.

"Hey, I shouldn't even be here. The governor of this state has put out an execution order on all Mormons, as you know, and word of this had probably already reached his ears," Porter said.

"I can't thank ya enough fer comin' down here and helpin' me out, helpin' the whole town out," Uzziah said.

"Someday, somebody should take care of Governor Boggs," Porter mentioned offhand.

"I didn't hear that. Now, go on back to Nauvoo and give the prophet my best."

"Maybe he shoulda included a mention of fire when he blessed us," Porter said.

"Yeah, well, we gotta die of somethin', right?"

Porter got up and Uzziah rose from the table. The two men hugged, and it ended in a lot of loud pats on the back, the way men usually end hugs.

"I wish yer were still in Nauvoo," Porter said.

"I do, too, but then there are other wishes which would come before that," Uzziah said.

They walked out of the house. It was early morning, and Sheriff Buck Laurie was waving from outside his barn.

"I still don't know how ya convinced Buck to get into one of his wife's dresses," Uzziah said.

"It weren't me, I could hear her back in their bedroom tellin' him to put on that dress or they wouldn't get out of town alive. I think he did it fer her," Porter said, chuckling.

"Well, as long as I'm in Jeff City, I will be glad to remind him of that day," Uzziah said, getting into the chuckling with Porter. "Ya still got that address, Vrain's Trading Post, that I gave ya?"

"Sure do, who knows, *Men make plans and God laughs.*"

"And laughs and laughs and laughs," Uzziah continued.

Porter mounted up and turned his mare to Uzziah.

"Hey, when's that foal due?" Uzziah asked.

"A few more months now, I can hardly wait."

"Ride it in good health," Uzziah said, and Porter turned the mare and rode out.

Uzziah waited till Porter was out of sight, then went in the barn, saddled up Shadow, and put the sawback saddle on Jenny, who seemed actually happy they were about to travel. After loading up Jenny he rode over to Sheriff Laurie's house. Jenny was better than a door knocker with her braying, she wasn't ready to stop just yet.

Buck and Bethany came out and they looked at Uzziah strangely.

"You're leaving, there's going to be a parade in yer honor this weekend," Buck said.

"It's in the honor of the sheriff's department, and I hear the Marshals Service will be sending someone to set up an office in Jeff City," Uzziah said.

"They are, and I think it will keep the vacuum that Gongloe left from fillin' up with riffraff," Buck said.

"I thought ya was gonna wait till spring to go back to the mountains," Beth said, a tear forming in her eye.

"'Bout that, what's the sheriff's office gonna do with that paddle wheeler they confiscated from Gongloe?"

"Nothin'," Buck said.

"I want it, if it's all right with ya?"

"It's yours, son, and good riddance to it."

Uzziah Ferguson O'Bannon had always had an interest in steam power, and from the time that the first steam engine had appeared in the Shenandoah Valley, he had hung around with the older men and boys who knew how to run them. The principle was simple—heat the water, use the steam to drive the engine—and he was sure it was the same on the vessel that he had boarded and started up the Missouri River.

The reason the big paddle boats didn't go up in the fall was their fear of getting locked in by the ice when it finally formed on the river. And yet, Uzziah wasn't worried about that. He'd use the wood stations that the big steamers use, and rid them of extra wood, and they wouldn't be coming up till spring. In the meantime, he would navigate the Missouri in the fall. Shadow and Jenny were warm in the stalls, which were just off the boiler room, and there was a little cabin that he could sleep in when he needed to tether up to the shore or an island. He would travel in style till the ice stopped him, then he would do as any mountain man would do—tough it out, and go home to his cabin in the Rockies.

5

Like all good ideas, this one, the one with the little paddle wheeler, had its negative side—the sound of the little steam engine that powered the dang thing. Its steady thump, thump, thump was like a signal being broadcast across the prairie. If Injuns were around, they would certainly pick up on the steady rhythm. It was almost primitive in its steadiness. And yet, leaving Jefferson City and heading upriver, Uzziah settled into a rhythm of his own.

He was constantly checking the pressure gauge and the water level, making sure he didn't run short of water was vital. Then, there was the wood. It seemed the further up the Missouri he got, the less wood was at the wood stations, which led Uzziah to imagine that since the big paddle wheelers weren't going, that the locals, be they Injuns or settlers, were taking the wood for their own use, which he heartily resented. Soon, if this kept up, he would have to find an island with some timber growth on it and do some wood chopping. He guessed

Gongloe had imagined the same thing, since there was a rather newish-looking axe aboard.

Uzziah noticed fairly soon that both Shadow and Jenny were getting restive. Jenny was thrashing about in her stall and Shadow was beginning to hit the walls with his powerful hooves. What he didn't need was them not being in their stalls, it was too dangerous. They could fall overboard, or unbalance the load and maybe even sink the little vessel. Uzziah remembered the big raft that Immanuel had stolen, as it were, from his own people, the Mandans. This paddle wheeler was twice the size of that, but still not that big.

Up ahead, he saw a rather large island, and he hoped it didn't join the banks on either side, but he couldn't see around it. He pulled in and tied up to a strong-looking tree, and before he released his friends, he had a walk around, which took nearly half an hour.

When he got almost back and was rounding a bend in the island where there was a copse of small trees, he saw an Injun, he wasn't sure what tribe, but he had taken Shadow from his stall and put a bridle on him, and was leading him off onto the island. He wished he'd brought his binoculars that he'd bought in Chicago, but they, alas, were in his saddle bags. He wasn't too worried that the Injun, whatever tribe he was from, was actually going to ride the big stallion. The Injun was in for a big surprise. No one but Uzziah could ride Shadow!

Then, without any fuse at all, the skinny little Injun just slipped up on Shadow's back. Uzziah could see the Injun leaning forward and talking into the ear of the stallion, and then the most amazing thing happened. The Injun simply rode off on Shadow, as if he were his own horse. There was no resistance, no fighting with the horse. Uzziah could see that the Injun had put a war bridle of horse hair on Shadow, and he was responding perfectly. It sure looked like Uzziah was about to lose a horse!

Uzziah raised up the Hawken and was aiming when the next amazing thing happened, the Injun rode Shadow straight toward Uzziah as if he knew he was standing behind that copse of small trees. Uzziah lowered the rifle, and within a minute, the Injun was sitting on his horse not twenty feet from where he thought he was hiding.

"You think you hide, but body too big," the Injun began, "I am the Mohawk George Henry Martin. My death takes me into the wilderness where the sounds of drums disturb my peace. Who are you?"

"Uzziah Ferguson O'Bannon."

"I like Irish because they like drink," George said, then added, "Have whiskey?"

"Yes, but how do you ride my horse?" Uzziah asked.

"I get on, I ride," was all George said as he dismounted and walked forward with the war bridle in his hand. Uzziah took it, and they walked back toward the paddle wheeler. He looked at the old man, who must have been really old. The skin hung from his bones, and he couldn't have weighed more than ninety pounds.

"My death disappoints me," George said.

"How's that?"

"It comes like a woman takin' her time."

Uzziah had scouted the land, and it was an island. He went and let Jenny out, who had been braying since

Shadow had been taken from his stall. He let her out and released them both to run the island.

George put a hand to his eyes to block out the sun and watched as they ran off.

"Magnificent," he said.

"How did ya learn yer English?"

"The English from the priests. First, we killed them, then they teach us."

"You speak well."

"I know," George said, still watching Shadow and Jenny buck and fart.

"Are you hungry?"

"Look at me, what do you think?"

Uzziah fixed breakfast because the eggs he had weren't going to last that long, and he wanted the old, evidently dying man to have a good last meal. He cooked on the island, although there was an ability to do so on the vessel. He made grits, sausage links, and his Dutch oven biscuits. They ate in silence, and Uzziah was amazed that someone that skinny could put the food away that he did.

"Now what?" George asked.

"You go back to yer dyin', I continue upriver, no?"

"No, death is boring. I go upriver," George said, and he walked over to where he had stored some jerked meat, his bow and arrows, and some other things, which Uzziah could not identify.

The old Mohawk was dressed in a breechcloth made of deerskin, with deerskin leggings, a deerskin shirt with arm and knee bands. He also had a quill and flint arrows in a hunting bag.

He settled himself close to the engine, where it was warm, and sat and looked at everything around him.

Oh well, Uzziah thought, *it will be nice to have company, and what harm can he do?*

He would find out later what harm an old man can do.

While they were moored to the island, Uzziah spent several hours chopping wood, and yes, it was green and it would smoke a lot, but he also found plenty of dried driftwood, sawyers which had snagged themselves on the island, and those he also chopped into pieces adequate for the firebox. When he was done, he looked over and George was lying down near the firebox.

Well, what do ya know, thought Uzziah, *the old man finally croaked!*

He walked over and started to pick George up so he could bury him.

"Not yet," George said.

They traveled like that for nearly a week. At five miles an hour going upstream and making as good a time as they could, Uzziah figured they just might be close to St. Joseph's on the Missouri.

As they traveled, he taught George how the steam engine worked, never too old for an old dog to learn a new trick, and he had the concept down. George might be old, but his mind was sharp and he learned well. Fairly soon, Uzziah could take naps and let George watch the gauges and feed the firebox. If anything untoward happened, George would wake him up.

Once Uzziah awakened, and there was George with his face into the wind, and what hair he had, they plucked most of it except for that band down the middle of his head. That band had grown long, and it was flying back away from his hawklike face, and the joy which Uzziah saw on that old Mohawk's face, well, it warmed the cockles of his heart.

George looked over, it was as if he knew that someone was watching him, and he smiled at Uzziah, then winked. Uzziah figured winking must be universal, and it stood for all kinds of shite. A woman winked at you, it meant one thing, a man winked at you, it might be a call to a fight, but this wink was conspiratorial. George was dying, but having a hell of a time doing it, and Uzziah was glad to be a part of the last days of this Mohawk's life.

One night, they were moored to another island and Shadow and Jenny were off in the distance. The only time you could see them was when their eyes would echo the iridescence back at you, reflecting the fire that George and Uzziah sat around.

"When I was young, we fought the French, then the British, and now, I think we fight the Americans. They are all White men and understand little. I saw brothers scalped for money, and sisters raped for what—joy? I think not. As I grew, I took a seat on many councils and rose in the eyes of my people, but leading is a disappointment much like death. Those who follow do so slowly, very slowly. My first wife gave me many children, but died when a child got stuck. After that, my love for them—the women—it waned a bit. They are strong but also fragile, this I do not understand. Either you are strong or fragile, but how to be both is a mystery to all men.

"Most White men are fools and more savage than any red man. You are nice for a change. Your dress suggests those who think Jesus was in the Americas—"

"You know the Mormons?"

"Yes, but they follow a boy's dream, which would have been interesting over a campfire in the winter, but nothing more. Yet, they are good mostly, and you have a wife?"

"How did you know?"

"The gold ring," George said, nodding in the direction of Uzziah's left hand.

Uzziah looked down at it and said, "Yes, we have three children, and she is beautiful."

George looked at Uzziah and shook his head.

"What's wrong, don't you believe me?" Uzziah asked.

"Of course, last two born in heaven, eh?" George offered, and Uzziah decided to let it go.

Uzziah wondered how some people could always tell when lies were being spoken, and yet this man, this Mohawk, had not insulted him by saying *you are lying*, he simply put it differently.

They could see the lights of Blacksnake reflected in the low clouds that were sitting over the town.

"I will hide," George said.

"Surely, that won't be necessary?"

"I will hide, someone will think I'm a ghost. Don't worry 'bout the animals or your things, no harm will come. I have enclosed all this in a dream," George said.

They docked short of Blacksnake, and in the morning, Uzziah moored where he was charged for the mooring, not much, but enough. He rode Shadow away, and much to his surprise, George was able to keep Jenny quiet. Jenny liked the dying Mohawk, and they often slept curled up together.

Uzziah had seen towns like this, they had the quality of shiftlessness about them. That was, they were made of establishments which were inside tents, and only later, when funds rolled in, could these establishments begin to look better established.

The first such business like that was owned by C.A. Perry and his brother, Elias H. Perry. They had, in fact, been merchants in St. Louis. When Uzziah walked into their rather large tent in search of supplies, a voice shouted out at him.

"Uzziah! My God, it can't be you?!?" It was Elias Perry, and before Uzziah knew it, the man's arms were around him, and he was fairly sure it wasn't a weapons check because everyone carried weapons.

"Elias?"

"You remembered, I'm flattered."

"What are ya doin' out this way, thought that business in St. Louis was doing well?"

"It was, it was, but like you, young man, we older men, we have the wanderlust, too, ya know, oh yes, we do."

As Elias was speaking, his brother came over. "This can't be the man who was wanted for"—and he lowered his voice—"the murder of the undersheriff, can it?"

"Charles, how are ya?" Uzziah asked.

"Well, believe me. We still have that store in St. Louis, where you and, what was his name?"

"Immanuel."

"Yes, yes, the two of you always shopped with us, and we appreciated your return business. We're about to erect a brick building here in Blacksnake. Come, come!" he said as he led Uzziah outside the tent. They walked through the mud, Uzziah holding onto Shadow's reins, and Charles Perry admiring the horse without saying anything.

"There!" he said as he walked up to some foundation work which had been laid, and there were pallets of bricks there, too.

"You aren't guarding the bricks?" Uzziah asked.

"Well, since no other buildings will have them, I think we will know if any are taken," Charles said and laughed uproariously.

"I'm gonna need some large items, but due to a windfall, I can afford it," Uzziah said.

"That's talk a merchant loves to hear," Charles said. "I hope we can accommodate you."

Once back at the tent store that would be moving to the brick building once it was completed, Uzziah spoke up.

"Need two buffalo coats with hoods, and a good solid horse," Uzziah said, not seeing any buffalo coats and certainly not seeing any horses.

"Come with me," Charles said as they walked to the back section of the tent, which was cut off from the front by a tent wall.

"How 'bout these?" Charles said, holding up two

buffalo coats, then pointing to a couple of horses inside the tent, "We don't get much call fer horses, and they ain't cheap," he said.

Uzziah pulled out his wad and paid for everything.

They walked back into the big tent, and Uzziah got everything else he could think that he might need. His excess of cash was due to the burial party the Mormons had had for all of Gongloe's men. Of course, their names would be written down and the bastards would be baptized later. They had been handsomely paid to protect him, and Porter felt Uzziah deserved half of the take.

On his way back to the docks, riding Shadow and holding the reins to a gated Morgan, Uzziah heard some men yelling, and a man with a flint arrow in his arm ran past him.

"Where in hell did that come from?!" his friend was asking as the other man and he were taking him to see a doctor, Uzziah supposed.

"Be careful, friend, arrows are jest droppin' outta the sky!" one of them said as they passed Uzziah.

When he got to the paddle wheeler, George came from the darkness.

"I tried telling them, but they boarded anyway," he said, his bow in his hand and flint arrows in his quiver.

"Well, I think we oughta go on upstream, don't know what kinda law, if any, they gots 'round chere," Uzziah said as he threw more wood in the firebox.

They didn't go far, they didn't have to in the dark. Settling in among the reeds on the other side of the

Missouri, they could hear shouting and hollering from the docks at Blacksnake, but paid them no mind as Uzziah fixed supper.

As they sat there after supper, listening to the commotion of Blacksnake, Uzziah started talking to George. That old Mohawk had a way of listening that relaxed Uzziah a lot.

He told him about him and Immanuel breaking up over the drinking and whoring, and about Nauvoo, and the love of his life, Hannah. At one point, Uzziah realized he was telling this old Injun more about himself than he ever told anyone. He even told of Porter Rockwell's blessing of him, how he could neither be touched by bullet or blade and that he was under God's protection!

He hadn't imagined he'd tell anyone about that. But then he remembered, there were times in life when you were not with your family, and maybe sitting in a place where you're waiting on a stage, a train, or just waiting for your life to resume. At those times, Uzziah remembered it was easy to tell someone with no investment in you about yourself. All your mistakes, and many faux pas, and some things you wouldn't think of telling family, but this person just happened to be there at the right time, and it was like being ripe with too much information, too much on your heart, and you were, in essence, low-hanging fruit for the other person's ear. And when all was said about what had been done, you felt better. Somehow relieved that it wasn't only you who knew these things, but another living soul, and if you chose righteously, you knew you weren't being judged.

They decided—well, Uzziah decided—that they

would head out early the next morning, and by the time the sun was reflecting off the river, they were out of sight of Blacksnake.

George kept working the firebox and making sure the steam was up, and the arrangement suited Uzziah, who took to hunting for game off the paddle wheeler. Game seemed plentiful, and making sure that both Shadow and Jenny were locked into their stalls, Uzziah laid on the pilot house floor where Gongloe had been taken and sighted in with his Hawken. Since it was a long-range rifle, he sighted in on game a good deal ahead of them, and close to the river, so they could simply pull over at that point and load the dead animal up.

Uzziah wanted to try out the Girandoni air rifle that they had found on one of the dead guards working for Gongloe. The rifle operated on an air system which allowed 20-30 shots without reloading, and there was the extra-added advantage of no significant report from the rifle and no smoke. Virtually undetectable by those you were shooting at.

Uzziah had fired it a few times with Porter, but he insisted that it would be of more use to his friend, Uzziah, than it would be to him. Then he confessed that the feel and sound of the air rifle were disappointing to him since he loved the smoke, recoil, and loud sounds of powder weapons.

The Girandoni came with its own system. The Girandoni system accouterments bag included a bullet mold, an air pump, spare air flasks, and wrenches.

6

As they approached Council Bluffs, George spoke up.

"Too many Indians here," he said.

"Whatcha mean?"

"All Indians from White man Chicago brought here. They not happy, fight each other."

They had plenty of meat from Uzziah's hunting, and so they traveled on, even though many along the shoreline beckoned them to come to shore. Uzziah thought of the sirens that had lured Ulysses. In Homer's Odyssey, Ulysses had his own sailors tie him to the mast so that he could resist the cry of the sirens, and they—the sailors—were ordered to stuff their ears in order so they could not hear the sirens' song. Still, Uzziah had wanted to stop at Council Bluffs, but getting embroiled in troubles between varying tribes that had been moved to reservations wasn't on his list of things to do.

There basically weren't any other stops along the way unless it was for wood or to refill the water for the steam engine, and even that could be done without stopping, just scooping the water from the river.

They traveled without incident for the next week. It seemed like the weather was cooperating, and even when it snowed, the winds didn't pick up. If this kept up, Uzziah could count himself one of the most blessed men ever.

He started to worry about what he would do if George didn't die before he got as far as he was going. Uzziah supposed he could take the elderly—elderly—hell, he was probably one of the oldest people Uzziah had ever dealt with. He mentioned things which happened easily eighty years ago, and they weren't when he was an infant. Like a lot of Injuns, George most likely didn't know his age.

"George," Uzziah spoke up early one morning, after they had unmoored from a tree along the northern bank of the river, "do you know how many years ya have on this earth?"

"Sure, nearly ninety-six years, will be ninety-six when the New Year arrives," he said without thinking that it was extraordinary.

"Why are you so sure?"

"My mother lived a long time, I think she was over 100 when she passed, and she told me my birthdate."

"I see," Uzziah said, and was about to say something else when he heard a native cry into the morning air. Looking over to the other bank, he saw a group of thirty-some Injuns riding along much faster than the paddle wheeler. None of them had rifles, some fired pistols, but at that range, most of the shots fell short.

"Stay on the firebox, and keep things in keel," he

said as he got out the Girandoni and checked the air pressure on it. It seemed fully charged.

"Are you going to kill my brothers?" George asked.

"Are they Mohawks?"

"No, Sioux, I believe."

"Then, no, I'm not going to kill yer brothers," Uzziah said as he lay down and opened fire with the air rifle.

As the Sioux began to fall from their saddles, it wasn't the number who fell that amazed the Sioux war party, it was the manner in which they were killed. All they could see was a man lying down on the floor of the pilot house holding something that neither made a sound nor caused smoke to float above the gun. When ten of their numbers had fallen, they stopped chasing the little paddle wheeler and circled back to their camp. But not before they sent someone to shout at the paddle wheeler in Sioux. He was young and obviously brave, and as he raised a war lance, he shouted many things, which neither George nor Uzziah could understand, then he rode away yipping all the way. When he joined the group, he said something to them, and they all rode away yipping and hollering.

"What ya suppose that was about?" Uzziah asked George.

George was pensive for a moment, then he spoke with a gravity which surprised Uzziah. "That weapon which makes no sound or smoke is big medicine to them. Big medicine."

"I explained it to you, didn't I?" Uzziah asked.

"Yes, but your explanation was meaningless till I saw the bodies fall as if by magic."

"Magic?"

"You pointed a stick at them and they died."

"Here," Uzziah said, holding the Girandoni air rifle out to George, who did not take it, but turned away, even refusing to look at it.

"That stick scares me, and if death wasn't chasing me, I would leave you now, but it isn't time," George said as he settled down to check gauges and mess with the dials.

Uzziah thought about what had just happened. He thought that since George spoke good English that George was somehow from his world, but he wasn't. The native mind was more like the mind of a child than that of the White man. Simple proof, in fact, the air rifle, which looked to them—both the Sioux and, it would seem, the Mohawk also—to be a death stick. No reloading, well, he hadn't made it through the requisite thirty rounds, and no smoke and no noise—a death stick.

He wished Porter were here and they could share their thoughts on the subject. When he rejoined Immanuel, whom he surely hoped was back at the cabins, they would talk of this death stick, and Immanuel would see it as a great boon for their travels. Wherever they went, all they had to do was point the death stick at Injuns, and those who fell testified to its medicine.

Word must have gotten around on the prairie as it always did, smoke signals, over the dead buffalo gossip, rumors spread by runners, who knew? But they saw plenty of Injuns after that, but they all kept their distance. It was as if they could not stay away, but also could not let the death stick be pointed at them. To test out this theory, Uzziah waited until a band of Crows, he believed it was, were riding not close, but not far away from the paddle wheeler.

Uzziah stood up and, yelling, he brandished the death stick over his head and pumped it up and down as if he were celebrating its medicine. The Crows scattered like they had been leaves blown in the wind, making shrieking noises, and yipping away, but none of them came closer, not a one!

From that time forward, they were not bothered by any of the tribes. And the white man thought he knew about communication?

From the north, clouds were gathering, and it looked like what they called a blue norther.

Uzziah went around and battened down everything that could blow away. They stopped at an island and he chopped an enormous amount of wood. It was stacked as high as the pilot house, and Uzziah worried about it blowing away. He took several large rocks he found on the island, and, throwing a tarp over the stacked wood, he weighed it down with the rocks. Surely that would hold.

He wasn't sure where they were on the river exactly, but if this storm brought the cold, which Uzziah imagined that it would, they would be riding horses after this, and the paddle wheeler would be frozen in the Missouri till the spring thaw came.

After chopping the wood, he and George went around and cut with their knives as much grass as was on the island. Uzziah hoped it would be enough. If the paddle wheeler got stuck, they would load the grasses on Jenny. It would look heavy, but the relative weight wouldn't be that much.

They got back into the vessel, fed the two horses

and Jenny as much grass as they could, then threw some oats in for good measure. The wind was already starting to make the American flag on the pilot house flap like there was no tomorrow, and maybe there wouldn't be. Uzziah made sure that the mooring rope, which was tied to a sturdy tree, was long enough that if the river rose because of the coming storm, there would be enough slack to handle the extra water.

George and Uzziah settled into the little cabin on the main deck and made supper, well, Uzziah made supper, as they prepared to wait out the storm.

Three days later, the storm had finally abated. Uzziah was worried about the horses and Jenny, and when he tried to leave the cabin, it took all his strength to open the door. The entire area around the island was covered with snow, you couldn't even see the Missouri. Uzziah imagined with the freezing air around him that it—the Missouri—had frozen over. He dug his way to the stalls, and Jenny started braying the minute she heard someone was coming.

It took him close to an hour to dig a path to the stalls. All the hay was gone, and going out to check on the extra hay and wood, Uzziah found that the tarp had been blown away, and so had the wood and grasses they gathered—so much for planning ahead. There were enough grasses left to feed all three of their animals, and a smidgen of wood to keep him and George warm that night.

The sky was crystal clear blue, and there were no clouds at all. The wind was nonexistent, and it was so bright that Uzziah wished he had thought to buy the smoked glasses Charles had shown him, but he hadn't.

That night, they stayed warm, for as everyone knows, the clear nights are the coldest with no blanket of clouds keeping the temperatures up as the heat of the earth gets reflected back to the earth.

That morning, all decked out in their buffalo coats, George looked like the coat was wearing him instead of the other way around. He said he was mighty warm though, and that was all that mattered.

They stacked what little grasses they could find on the ship on top of the sawbuck saddle, and the gaited Morgan turned out to be the perfect horse for George. She was small, fourteen hands, and she couldn't have had a better disposition. When you got off her, you had to watch your feet because she would come right up next to you, wanting to be close.

The first day, they rode far enough away, following the sun as it went west, until finally, they could no longer see the mast of the Paddle wheeler.

Uzziah found a small stream that was frozen over, but could be broken with the butt of a pistol, and he made supper under a copse of cottonwood trees. He didn't worry about the smoke because he imagined that no self-respecting Injun would be found out in the weather they were in.

The next few days went as if scripted, the same following of the sun, and on the sunset of the third day, they saw the sun sinking behind the Rockies.

Uzziah dismounted, got on his knees, put his hands together, and thanked Father for bringing him back to where he belonged. When he stopped silently praying, George was kneeling beside him.

"You trackin'?" George asked. "Don't see no sign."

You had to hand it to the Mohawk, he had himself a sense of humor.

They made camp, and it also seemed as if the area that the storm had affected was lessening—the prairie ahead looked like it barely had any snow on it at all.

The seventh day out from the Missouri, they ran across a hunting party of Blackfeet and they rode fast toward them, yelling and screaming until Uzziah raised the Girandoni air rifle over his head and yipped back at them. They pulled their war bridles up and came no closer, but had a meeting about what to do next. It seemed they must have heard about the death stick, but maybe the tribe they heard it from was pulling their proverbial leggings.

Finally, one rider rode like the wind toward them, of course, screaming and yipping at the top of his lungs. It was, of course, a young buck.

Uzziah raised the Girandoni air rifle, cocked the mechanism, and fired a smokeless and essentially noiseless shot. The brave flew back off his horse, dead.

The remaining war party did a double-take, then, not bothering to gather the body of the young brave who had been killed by the death stick right before their eyes, rode off.

Uzziah imagined that was the end of all Injun troubles, and it was.

7

Uzziah and George rode into the Vrain Trading Post, and that decided one thing, Immanuel had been there earlier, months earlier. So, that much was decided.

George had fun shopping, and he spent almost his entire time at the trading post in front of the candy counter. He picked several hard candies from the glass-covered counter and was thrilled when he put the first piece into his mouth. Not having many teeth, he sucked the first piece, and Uzziah watched as an expression of contentment came over the old Mohawk's face.

"This is better than whiskey," George said, and he meant it.

Uzziah figured if Immanuel hadn't been there in a couple months he would need coffee, sugar, flour, bacon, tobacco, and the other staples. He got a portion of each, figuring they would be feeding three for some time. Jenny had plenty of room on her back, and the packages they gathered and took out and tied on the sawbuck were hardly noticeable to her. Before Uzziah knew what George was doing, he had handed a piece of hard candy to both Shadow and Jenny.

Their chewing started out slowly, then as the sugar melted in their mouths, saliva began to roil from their mouths, and when they were done, Shadow was pulling back his lips and smiling while Jenny was kicking out her feet as if this would bring her more of what George had given her. When that didn't work, she began an incessant braying, which was accompanied by guttural whinnying from Shadow that Uzziah was sure he'd never heard before. The two of them sounded like a crazed duet of sugar-happy equines, and both Uzziah and George laughed as each of them began in again as soon as they were finished with the last treat.

The rest of the ride up to the cabins was easy, really. Uzziah had so many memories flooding back upon him, then remembering the things that had happened to him since leaving Immanuel on the big paddle wheeler, he was perplexed as to where he would begin, if, and it was a real *if,* Immanuel were there. He had been known to go off in the past. When they got back from Nuevo Mexico and his being buried alive, Immanuel had taken off for a great deal of time before he came riding back in. Uzziah didn't know what to expect.

Uzziah and George hardly talked at all once they got into the Rockies. There was George's first wonder at such tall and majestic mountains, then he could hear George behind him praying away, or was he singing? He wasn't sure. He had almost forgotten that when he found George, or George found him, that the man was angry at his death for having taken so long to come to him, maybe he was singing his death song as many Injuns did, Uzziah simply didn't know. He had hoped to get to the cabins before sunset, but it was winter, and the ole globe went behind the Rockies fairly fast in its short circle that time of year.

It may have been dark, but Uzziah had ridden this path a hundred times in his dreams, not to mention the thousands of times in real life. When they got fairly close, he could see the ambient light reflected from the ponderosas and the clouds that were over the cabins. Someone was there!

Now, in the mountains, it is always assumed that if a cabin is left uninhabited, well, then any old mountain man is welcomed to use it as long as he left it in the same shape that he found it in, but when Uzziah finally rode up on that last ridge and looked, what he saw amazed him.

Someone had rebuilt two of the cabins completely. The barn was redone, and he heard the snort of a horse who had obviously heard their coming.

"Is this yer place?" George asked softly.

"Yeah, gots to be careful, don't know who might be chere," Uzziah said.

They tied the horses and Jenny, by God, Jenny had not brayed, and that made Uzziah wonder even more. Perhaps there was danger in the cabins, perhaps her non-braying itself was a warning?

Uzziah asked George to hold the reins of the gated Morgan that George was calling China—because he'd heard the name once, and liked it—and Shadow's reins, too.

Uzziah snuck up on both lit cabins, and the one on

the right, his old cabin, was the source of a conversation. Well, if it was Immanuel, he had obviously found another partner, and Uzziah was willing to go on his own way, if that's what the older man wanted.

He stood at the door to his old cabin and looked back. There was Jenny's snout sniffing the air. He should have known she would follow him, especially since the discovery of hard candy back at the Vrain! Tuning back to the cabins, he eavesdropped as best he could.

"Well, young son," Immanuel said, there was no mistaking his voice, "that's the way I feels 'bout it, how 'bout ya?"

"Yer wrong, acourse," the other voice said accusatorially, and Uzziah, for the life of him, had heard that voice before, but where? The other voice continued, "Like always ya got into the whiskey afore ya got into yer mind, and ya don't really have a notion what yer thinkin' right now!"

By God, whoever was giving Immanuel hell had it right, he had it righteously right. He had said as much to his partner many times before, and it seemed this new partner had centered in on Immanuel's problems, right quick.

"Young son, ya wouldn't be alive if it weren't fer me, who saved all our bacons back when we was at the buffalo run, huh? Who rode out to make the deal with the medicine man of the Blackfeet, who, huh, who!?" Immanuel was being insistent, but he was Immanuel's partner up at the buffalo run, who else was there, who would remember such? Well, there was Beckwourth! That was it, Immanuel and Beckwourth had finally joined forces, which meant that Beckwourth's handsome Crow wives would be in the other cabin. He had some wonderful bedroll encounters with one or more of Beckwourth's wives, and he swore he couldn't tell them apart!

He lithered over to the other cabin door and listened for female sounds. He wasn't quite sure what female sounds were, unless you were in the bedroll with one of them, and just the thought of those sounds made his Johnson swell. And yet, there were no sounds coming from Immanuel's cabin, and the louder conversation in his old cabin drowned out everything. Danm! That Immanuel was loud when he was in his cups. Uzziah slipped back over to his old cabin and nearly tripped over Jenny, whose nose was nearly in his pockets looking for candy.

At that cabin, before the other man could answer, Uzziah heard a cork come off a bottle and the guzzling of whiskey. This other man could only be someone who was with them at that buffalo run, and except for Oscar, who had died there, and Beckwourth, the only other white man was Willet, Oscar's brother, and it didn't sound nothing like him.

"Okay, okay, okay, ya done saved our bacons and fer the umpteenth time, ya want credit fer it, don't ya, don't ya?" the voice said, and it hit Uzziah where he'd heard the voice before!

He heard it when he and Immanuel were reading Shakespeare in the middle of the last winter they'd spent together. It was one of the voices that Immanuel used for some of the Bard's lesser characters. Damn it, Immanuel had done lost his ever-living mind and was talking to himself.

It was too embarrassing, he couldn't knock on the

door and catch his insanely lonely partner talking as if he were another man. Uzziah made up his mind, he and George would ride up to the highland meadow and sleep there, then come back down when the day was good into itself, and Immanuel was likely to be sober—emphasis on likely.

As he turned, Jenny had made up her mind that it was time for them to go to the barn and eat some real hay, she brayed and it almost blew Uzziah's Mormon hat off his head.

"Who's that!" It was Immanuel. Uzziah could hear the Hawken cocking. He and Jenny ran for the edge of the woods. "I said who the hell is out there! Ifn ya don't announce, I shall assume ya are an enemy who needs to be dispatched." The front door of Uzziah's old cabin opened. The light caught both George and Uzziah by surprise and they couldn't see a thing, but then again, neither could Immanuel, who had been sitting and drinking in all that brightness!

Thankfully, Jenny had stopped braying, and George, China, Uzziah, Shadow, and Jenny had pulled themselves back into the timber, and as it always happened, those who come from the fire cannot see into the night.

Immanuel started swearing a string of expletives that would have made anybody blush.

"He good swearer," George whispered into Uzziah's ear.

Uzziah motioned for him to be quiet, and they walked back down the hill as Immanuel fired the Hawken after imaginary uninvited guests. Good thing they hadn't stayed near the cabins, when that man drank, he could be dangerous, and that's all there was to it.

They camped up in the highland meadow, the same place where Immanuel and he had camped when they couldn't stay at their cabins in fear that bounty hunters would come after them. They had a cold camp, ate jerked meat, and drank water from the creek, which still ran free in the middle.

In the morning, Uzziah fixed a normal breakfast for him and George, as the horses and Jenny ate from beneath the snow to the shoots of grass which had been covered up.

They rode down to the camp, and as they were coming down the hill, Uzziah made a point of making a lot of noise and even singing his favorite hymn, *Rock of Ages*! He was caught off guard when George chimed in with the harmony and had an amazingly good voice! The priest had done good work on George.

When they made the cabins, Immanuel was standing in the middle of the cabin yard and looking up the hill as if he was going to see a ghost.

"What in God's name has the cat dragged in?" Immanuel shouted and ran toward Shadow, who balked a bit, but it didn't faze Immanuel. He grabbed ahold of his partner's leg and hung on as Shadow dragged him all over the cabin yard. Immanuel was hollering the whole time, which did not encourage Shadow to settle down, and finally, when he stopped yelling and Shadow calmed down a bit, Uzziah looked down on his partner.

"Well, old son, how are things with yer soul?"

Immanuel could not speak, he put his hands to his head and spun around in the cabin yard, and each time he looked back at Uzziah, he shook his head and did another spin.

"He okay?" George asked, and for the first time, Immanuel saw the skinny Injun wrapped in a coat that probably weighed more than he did.

"Who the hell are you!?!" Immanuel asked George.

"He's George," Uzziah said.

"I'm George," George said at basically the same time as Uzziah spoke.

"More like a voice in a buffalo robe," Immanuel said, then looked between the skinny Injun and his old partner, then back and forth again.

"How come yer ridin' *down* the mountain?" Immanuel asked, still smiling, but confused.

"We stayed up on the high meadow last night," Uzziah said.

"Oh...oh, that was you and George last night, were it?"

"Whatcha mean?"

"I heard Jenny, and there she is," and on cue, Jenny brayed and walked over to the barndoor. "It were Jenny I heard, and then comin' out couldn't see shite, and ya left, why?"

"Hey, are ya gonna ask us in or what? It's still winter, last time I checked," Uzziah said, hoping Immanuel would drop the whole *why didn't you knock last night thing*.

"Yeah, yeah, yeah, sure. Put the hosses away, and throw some grass feed, there's plenty, and y'all come on in, *my cabin*!" Immanuel made a point of which cabin they were to enter.

"Don't let that devil of a hoss back in the barn, scare ya! I got a big bet says he can outrun Shadow."

Uzziah and George put up the horses, and Jenny was so relieved when the sawbuck came off, she brayed till they were almost deaf, but it gave George time to ask questions.

"Your partner, he okay?"

"Yeah, yeah, just surprised to see us."

"Maybe I should leave?" George said.

"And go where?" Uzziah asked, seeing the iridescent glow of a large horse's eyes in the back of the barn.

"I could just freeze, then death couldn't escape me," George said and smiled.

"Nah, come on in with me."

When they came from the barn, which had been expanded, Immanuel was still in his shirtsleeves with the door to his cabin open. Uzziah was carrying his saddlebags and some other things he wanted to put in his cabin. When he started to walk past Immanuel, an arm went out.

"Just put 'em in my cabin, we can change things 'round later," Immanuel said, smiling a smile which Uzziah remembered to be his sneaky smile.

"O-kay," Uzziah said, and once he and George were inside Immanuel's cabin and it was warm in there, they stripped down by taking off their buffalo coats and gear, and Immanuel looked between George and Uzziah.

"He's dressed like we dress. Who ya dressed like?" Immanuel asked, looking at the Mormon garb of a broadcloth black coat, suspendered pants, and no vest with a white shirt bright beneath the coat.

"Myself," was all Uzziah said, and turned to George, "Ya want some coffee?"

George had a cup along with Immanuel, and the three men sat around the fire like they were waiting on a train to arrive and they really didn't know each other. Finally, both Immanuel and Uzziah spoke at the same time, and they said exactly the same thing.

"Whatcha been up to?" Immanuel and Uzziah said together, then they both laughed.

"You sure you know each other?" George asked.

"Who are you again?" Immanuel asked none too friendly-like.

"I'm waiting on death, he shouldn't be too far behind," George said as he sipped his coffee.

That remark got Immanuel thinking of what the Crow had said to him at Vrain Trading Post, something about death following him, wasn't it?

"What's that supposed to mean?" Immanuel asked with an edge to his voice.

"It mean my death has been following me, but refuses to come close," George said as he sipped his hot coffee, thinking nothing about what he was saying.

Immanuel looked away, not sure if the old Injun was death himself. Well, he was recovering from a pretty hard night at the bottle. He turned his attention to Uzziah.

"Ya look good, if not different," Immanuel said to Uzziah.

"Ya lost at least a hundred pounds, what happened?" Uzziah asked his skinnier partner.

"Decided I needed to get slimmer," Immanuel lied.

"Bullshit!" Uzziah said, calling a spade a spade.

"Still, ya look good," Immanuel said, turning the conversation on Uzziah.

"And ya look like hell warmed over," Uzziah said,

and George spat the coffee that he was drinking clear into the fire.

"This arsehole always speaks the truth," Immanuel said to George as if it were necessary to explain.

"Immanuel, are ya all right?" Uzziah asked.

"Course I'm all right, why wouldn't I be all right, whatcha askin' a question like thataone fer?"

"I'm a bit worried 'bout ya, that's all," Uzziah said.

"Well, well, worried is ya, worried, well, ya wasn't worried 'nuff to stay with me and I had—well what the hell ya leave me fer!?!" Immanuel asked.

"Ya know why."

"Yeah, I do."

"Well, I'm gonna put my stuff up and start a fire in my cabin," Uzziah said as he started to get up.

"Ah, so now, that other cabin's yourin, is it?"

"Well, used to be."

"Used to be's are plentiful around these parts, *young son,*" Immanuel said, and Uzziah couldn't believe that the phrase that he had wanted to hear from his old partner all this time had come out at him like it was an accusation.

"Well, lessin' all us gonna sleep in chere, I gots to start a fire in there—"

"Fire's agoin'."

"Waste a wood, wouldn't ya say?"

"My wood to waste, don't recall ya helpin' fell it, chop it, or bring it in." Immanuel's jaw was set like he was ready for a fight.

"Still, I'm goin' next door to the cabin which I used to occupy and put some of the things away which are crowding us up chere," Uzziah said as he stood, and Immanuel stood with him.

George had seen enough men fight in his long life to know that this was the beginning of one, and that was for sure! Both men had bowed up a bit, and that was usually a sure sign.

As Uzziah picked up his saddlebags and went for the door, Immanuel stood in his way. The two men were as close as they ever got with each other, and Uzziah wondered what the heck was going on, what was Immanuel hiding in his old partner's cabin? Maybe there was a girl in there and Immanuel didn't want to share. Maybe, well, he didn't know maybe what? He took another step and Immanuel pushed him back!

George took his coffee and moved to the corner of Immanuel's cabin.

"Ya ain't goin' in there, partner."

"But, I am...I am goin' in that cabin which used to be mine!"

"It ain't yers no more!" Immanuel shouted and took a swing at Uzziah, but he had forgotten, Uzziah was still younger, and Immanuel had left his right side exposed when the punch he intended for Uzziah had swished over the younger man's head. Uzziah nailed Immanuel right in his brisket, on the ribs, and as hard as he ever hit anyone.

The breath went out of his older partner, and he grabbed at his chest and thought for a moment his pigheadedness had caused him to have another angina pectoris. He could not breathe, just like the night on the gambling paddle wheeler, and he went down in a wheezing heap.

Uzziah stepped over Immanuel and started for the door when a hand reached out and grabbed his boot.

"Don't go in there, I beg ya, don't go in there," Immanuel got out between wheezes.

"Why not?" Uzziah looked down, giving his partner one last chance to explain.

"Just don't!" Immanuel wheezed.

Uzziah jerked his boot away from Immanuel's hand and went through the door of his partner's cabin, shutting the door behind him, and walked the short distance to what used to be his cabin.

"Don't!!" Immanuel screamed one last time.

Uzziah didn't know what he was going to find when he opened that door, but now, there was no way—unless an angel stood there with a flaming sword—that he wasn't going to go in there and see for himself! He opened the door and was greeted by a most pleasant sight. It was almost as if Immanuel had been in his cabin in Nauvoo. Someone had hung curtains around the windows. The chairs in there and the table were freshly made in the last year, and the fire was going ablaze, just like someone lived there. When he closed the door, he saw what all the fuss was about, and dropped everything he had in his hands.

Back in Immanuel's cabin, George walked away from the corner he'd been trying to disappear into, the place where he'd hoped not to get in the middle of a fight between two mountain men, but with Immanuel still flat out on his back and Uzziah having left, he decided he would join Uzziah. He went for the door, and Immanuel reached for his ankle. George was a lot faster than Immanuel could have imagined. He pulled the ankle away and went to the door.

"Where ya goin' Injun!?!" Immanuel asked, finally getting his breath back.

"You know," was all George said, and Immanuel sure enough knew.

The door to Uzziah's was closed, so he knocked, and he heard a voice from inside, "Come on in."

He walked in, and Uzziah's saddlebags and other articles he'd been carrying were right inside the door, and the mountain man was sitting at a newly made table. George came and sat with him.

"I don't get it," George said, and Uzziah pointed to the rocking chair in front of the fireplace.

"Oh," was all George said as he took it all in.

Evidently, someone had stuffed rags into clothes, deerskin pants, a shirt, and boots. The head was crudely made of a sack, which was stuffed with rags, and hanging from the front of the *face* was a whole lot of horse hairs to make a beard. *Eyes had been drawn in, and the face was really quite expressive,* George thought.

The hands were work gloves also stuffed, and in one hand was a tin mug which was sewn in place with the thumb and forefinger joined in the cup handle.

There was a knocking at the door. George looked at Uzziah, who looked at the door. The knock came again. Uzziah looked at the dummy in the rocking chair, and getting up, crossed the few feet to the door and opened it. There stood Immanuel with a shite-eating grin on his face.

"I can explain," he said sheepishly, looking at the dummy.

8

They sat there, the four of them, well, three, if you didn't count the dummy, and Immanuel looked at Uzziah, then back at George as if he were sending some signal to his partner.

"Look, he knows more about my life in the last year or so than anyone, so pay him no mind," Uzziah said, reaching over and patting George on the hand. George didn't react, he simply sat there staring past the dummy into the fire.

"It gets lonely up chere," Immanuel said, and Uzziah nodded in agreement.

"And?" Uzziah asked politely.

"Well, fer the past ten years I had ya to talk to, to wrastle with when I got ornery, to laugh with when things were funny. I tried goin' up to see Max and Fredrick, but they just wanted to drink my booze and talk loud 'bout stuff I couldn't care less 'bout. Ya know that fool Max is still missin' the whore he went over the falls with, the one that cost him his teeth?!"

Uzziah just kept looking at Immanuel, not knowing

what to say, and worrying about the sanity of his partner.

"Anyways, when I was redoin' yer cabin, ya noticed how nice it looks, don't ya?"

"Yeah, like ya was expectin' some some soiled dove to move in or somethin'!"

"Know what ya mean, it's the damned curtains, went overboard there, didn't I?"

He didn't wait for an answer, just kept with his tumbling speech, "So, I find some of yer ole clothes, a pair of deerskins when ya was thinner, not that yer fat, mind ya, and I started talking to the clothes like they was you, but they was just yer old clothes on the rockin' chair."

"Ya were talking to my ole clothes?" Uzziah asked with a tint of sarcasm, "And then what?"

"Then, one night when I'd gone down and gotten some bonded at Vrain's, I thought those clothes would look good ifn they was stuffed with rags and such, and then, I got the horsehairs from Trevor, and did ya notice the other horse way back in the barn?"

"Not really," Uzziah said.

"Really!?!"

"I saw his eyes reflecting the light," Uzziah admitted.

"That's a sure-fire story, I tell you, when I was in New Orleans—"

"Yer gettin' off topic," Uzziah reminded Immanuel.

"Well, hell, I don't care what time of the day 'tis, I gots to have a whiskey ifn I'm baring my soul," he said, and left Uzziah's cabin and went to his.

"He loves you, don't he," George said more than asked.

"We're close," Uzziah said, and Immanuel returned with a bottle and three glasses.

He held up the glasses and motioned, asking if they wanted drinks. Both men nodded that they did.

"It's starting to come down like cotton from the sky, looks like we might be in store fer a blizzard," Immanuel said, downing the first couple fingers and pouring himself another, before he'd poured a drink for Uzziah or George. The other two had empty glasses in their hands, and Immanuel hastily poured whiskey into them, spilling more than he got in the glasses.

"Uzziah, I missed ya, I thought ya'd be here when I got back, and I thought maybe when ya wasn't cherer, I'd ne'r see ya again, ne'r see ya again," he repeated with a certain hollowness in his voice. "Ya know?"

"Well, there was a reason I didn't make it back sooner, be glad to tell you as soon as you finish," Uzziah said.

"Finish, what the hell ya want from me, I said I missed ya, I made a damned dummy to take yer place, and I talked to the son of a bitch, I read Shakespeare with him, we told stories together, and we laughed a lot, but that don't mean I got the cabin fever, or that I lost my ever-lovin', fucking mind. Why ya puttin' me through this bullshit anyway? And why the fuck weren't ya here when I got back!?!"

"First off, I like what ya done to the place," Uzziah said as he looked around, "After the dynamite, it needed a redo, ya put some really nice touches to it," Uzziah said, rolling his eyes a little.

"Ya son of a bitch! I'll touch ya ifn ya start in that-away!" Immanuel said and took another shot.

"I got married," Uzziah said, and the change in Immanuel's face was a study in disbelief.

Then he recovered and started back in with his acid words. "She leave ya already, Uzziah? Is that what she done? Couldn't stand to be 'round yer fat arse!"

"Yes, she left."

"Bet ya didn't know how to treat her, did ya? We mountain men ain't meant to be married, yer the one convinced me of that, we're free spirits and all womens is ours."

"I treated her fine."

"Uh-huh, sure ya did, showed her a real good time, let her play with the lint in yer navel, did ya?"

At that moment, Uzziah remembered how Hannah had tested the depth of his navel and laughed when most of her finger disappeared.

"She died givin' birth to our son," Uzziah said, his head drooping a bit.

"Ya got a boy!" Immanuel said, ready to be proud of his younger partner.

"Gone."

"Dead?"

"Right after being borned."

They sat there, Immanuel sorry he'd gotten all hot and bothered about the dummy, who was the dummy now? What could he say? He just spat something out.

"Damn, young son, got dealt from the bottom of the deck, didn't ya?"

"No, it was a straight deal. Just sometimes, the cards are agin ya."

"Where'd ya meet her?"

"She was a Mormon."

"A what?"

"A Latter-Day Saint," Uzziah tried to explain.

"The bastards that have been chased all over from New York to Missouri?"

"If you've just read the papers, ya don't know nothin'," Uzziah offered.

"I know that that so-called prophet could have made hisself a million dollars ifn he'd put his mind to somethin' besides golden plates, and angels!" Immanuel said and took another shot of whiskey. He was on his favorite subject now, man's ability to bilk other men in the name of God.

"He's the one that did the weddin' ceremony fer Hannah and me."

"Nice name, always liked that name." Immanuel was pensive for the moment.

"Joseph Smith may or may not be a prophet, but he's a great man, and wherever he goes, towns spring up, and temples are built!"

"Then why are they chased all over kingdom come?"

"Same reasons the early Christians were fed to lions by the Romans."

"They're a bunch of lily-livered self-righteous no goods, without a thought of their own in their heads."

"Not Porter Rockwell," Uzziah said.

"Who the hell is he? Another Moron?"

"That's one of the favorite names people use when they try to discredit us," Uzziah remembered in Jefferson City being called such.

"So...he yer new hero, is he?" Immanuel asked, knowing this man had somehow caught Uzziah's imagination, which probably meant Immanuel was a has-been, a former hero of the young son.

"If ya could just meet him, Immanuel," Uzziah began, sitting forward and trying to convey the man's steel and image, "He's the bravest man I ever met, and we, the two of us, took down an entire gang of robbers, extortionists, and whore mongers when we was in Jefferson City."

"How'd ya do that?"

"Tell him the blessing," George spoke up, and for the first time, Uzziah wished that he hadn't included George in all this.

"What blessin'?" Immanuel jumped on the forbidden topic like a frog on a June bug.

"It's nothin' really," Uzziah said.

"No, no, it's how you fought all those desperadoes and lived, right? Tell me 'bout this godamned blessing, tell me!" Immanuel shouted.

"It ain't like that, it's holy," George said, believing in the blessing wholly, entirely.

"Is George gonna tell me, or are ya?" Immanuel asked, taking another shot straight from the bottle.

"I know how it'll sound to ya," Uzziah said, still thinking that there might be a way around telling Immanuel something that special to him.

"I tell, if you like?" George offered, and Uzziah thought, what a wonderful old man, willing to tell the blessing which wasn't even his.

"No, no, I'll tell," Uzziah said, knowing all along that with Immanuel in this drunken mood, the blessing would get besmirched forever.

"'Bout time," Immanuel said and looked at the bottle, but didn't take a drink.

"The prophet blessed Orin Porter Rockwell with these words, '*Orin Porter Rockwell, so long as ye shall remain loyal and true to thy faith, fear no enemy. Cut not thy hair and no bullet or blade can harm thee,'* Uzziah finished the blessing just as Porter had told him about it.

Immanuel's reaction was delayed, but when it came, it came with a vengeance. It came with all the vitriolic speech which Immanuel wanted to spew upon Uzziah's new hero, it came as a curse so that Uzziah would know what a fool he had been to believe such hogwash, and when the derisive laughter was over, Immanuel drew his pistol and pointed it straight at Uzziah's heart.

"Let's test the blessin', shall we?" he said and pulled back the hammer. As his finger pressured the trigger, Uzziah stood his ground, knowing that if it didn't work he'd be withi his son and wife, Hannah, and as the shot went off, there was a flash of something which passed between Immanuel and Uzziah and when the smoke cleared, George, the 96-year-old Mohawk lay on the floor, a hole in his chest and his life's blood leaking out.

"George, my friend, oh no!" Uzziah said as he pressed his bandana against the mortal wound.

Immanuel stood there looking down at the old Mohawk and then looked at his smoking weapon.

"Uzziah, I—" was all he was able to get out.

"I know I find death with you," George said, his hands holding the bandana against his bleeding wound.

"No, no, it isn't supposed to be like this!" Uzziah protested.

"Remember his words, 'Greater love hath no man—'" He looked surprised as he seemed to be looking beyond the ceiling of the cabin, then both his hands dropped away from the bloody cloth, and Uzziah stood up and looked at Immanuel, who pointed back at the dead body.

Uzziah looked. George's body had made a bloodied crucifix on the floor.

The blizzard lasted for three days, at the end of which, Uzziah retrieved George's body, frozen stiff from the snows outside his cabin. He had worried at first about some varmint getting the body before he could bury George the way he wished to be.

The night on the little paddle wheeler, when Uzziah had told George about all the things he never expected to tell another human being, George had felt free to tell Uzziah about the things that he wasn't proud of, and the things that had affected him the most in life. Odd, how those things that both men remembered were, in a very real sense, things that traversed the lines of ethnicity, the borders which the world considered so important as to put one man in one place and another man in another place.

Confessed truths about their lives ran across those imaginary borders and colors of skin. They had both lied to friends, cheated on their women, been less than brave at moments of great chance, and both had loved and hated deeply, forgiven things and been forgiven, both had wondered about their place in the greater scheme of things, and how their gods would react when they showed up on the other side. And yet, with George dead, Uzziah knew when he crossed over not only would Hannah and his son be there, but so would George, thankful again for the part Uzziah had played in his belated death, and thankful he could play a part in delaying Uzziah's demise.

The first few days of no snow, Uzziah had found a good two pieces of wood and carved them into ornamental sections, which he dovetailed together to make a cross. It mattered not what George believed, what matter was his recalling for Uzziah the verse from John 15:13—*Greater love hath no man than this: to lay down his life for one's friend.*

Uzziah had only taken the old Injun onboard as a lark, he was lonely and wanted some company for the trip up the Missouri. What he had done was no different than Immanuel's stuffing the clothes of his missing partner, so that he might not feel the lack of companionship. Neither had done anything wrong, though both felt they had. If onlys kept going through both of their minds, and Uzziah hadn't seen Immanuel since the day of the shooting.

When the cross was finished, Uzziah took his pickax and the body of the old Mohawk and traveled up to the highland meadow. There was a perfect spot for the burying of George Henry Martin.

Uzziah took the better part of the day just pickaxing through the permafrost, and once down to where there was actual loose dirt, he dug down a good six feet or so. The sun was shining nicely, and the body of his friend was supple. He had dressed him in his own deerskin shirt, which didn't have a bullet hole in it, a bullet hole which had been meant for Uzziah.

And as he was digging and preparing the last resting place of this Mohawk warrior, Uzziah kept thinking about two others he had buried earlier that year. How was it that this old Injun's death was reaching down as far into him as the deaths of his wife Hannah and his son, whom he decided he would always call George. How was it that death, no matter how random, how incidental, no matter how not a part of one's life, really, still was death.

We are sent here to this earth, which God so loved he gave his only Son, we are sent here from heaven, and some of us are known before we're born into this veil of tears, known as it says in Paul's book to the Romans, *For those God foreknew, he also predestined to be conformed to the likeness of his son, that he might be the firstborn among many brothers.*

Yes, he and George were brothers, as were he and Immanuel, and he wished Immanuel would come from his cabin and be with him in this, but he figured he had stayed drunk since the *accidental* shooting. As he was thinking thusly, he heard hoofbeats in the background, and when he turned, there was Immanuel, *God with us*, dressed as he would have been back in New Orleans. He was resplendent in his tailed coat, ruffled shirt, and gleaming riding boots, a sporty chapeau sat atop his head. And the horse he rode looked like a horse that had been made to be Shadow's companion for life. The two horses sniffed each other's muzzles, and the great black, which stamped next to Shadow, snorted and was answered by his brother in horseflesh.

Immanuel got down, tied the reins to his black horse to the saddle horn, took the ground tie of Uzziah, and did the same with Shadow's reins. The two horses took off into the meadow, testing each other's speed, and they seemed evenly and equally matched.

Immanuel picked up George's body, and it looked like a small child in the big man's arms. Immanuel looked at the vertical hole which Uzziah had dug and turned his head, for it was like no other grave he had ever seen.

"Standing in the grave, Mohawk way," Uzziah said.

Immanuel took the still firm body and set it up in the hole in a standing position, and Uzziah took the branches he'd woven and wedged them into the hole, so the dirt would not compress itself on the standing body. Then, both men took turns filling in the dirt till there was a pile on top that was about waist high.

Uzziah took the cross he'd made and pounded it into the top of the dirt pile. Burned on the crossbar of the cross were these words:

George Henry Martin
Mohawk Warrior
Friend of Immanuel & Uzziah

No words were spoken, there were no words. The two men looked at each other, and Immanuel smiled a bit. Uzziah grabbed him and held him close as both men tried not to weep, then the running about of the stallions got their attention, and Immanuel whistled for his black, who came over, and naturally, Shadow came with him.

"Stygian the Great," Immanuel said, gesturing to the horse. Stygian snorted and reared up, and Shadow, not to be undone, did the same.

Uzziah nodded his head as both men mounted up and galloped over the meadow, their long hair blowing in the racing breeze. They turned and looked at each other when both stallions had extended out to their full strides.

A LOOK AT BOOK SEVEN: THE PROMISED LAND
A UZZIAH MOUNTAIN MAN WESTERN DOUBLE

Faith leads them west. Trouble never stays behind.

When Uzziah O'Bannon and Immanuel Jones receive a message from the settlement, they ride to Vrain Trading Post and soon find themselves enlisted by Porter Rockwell, bodyguard to the late Joseph Smith. With the Mormon prophet killed, the remaining followers must be guided west to the Great Salt Lake. Along the trail lie hardship, sickness, and loss—including an attack by Comanches and the long-awaited burial of Hannah and baby George in a highland meadow.

After a punishing winter in the Rockies, the two mountain men are drawn south when a Texas cattle drive falters. The Great Northern Cattle Company sends 1,500 longhorns north from Fort Belknap, but dying cattle and dead men bring the drive to the edge of collapse. Uzziah and Immanuel step in to help.

The journey continues by river, but more lives are lost along the way. In Wolf Point, trail boss Ned "Texas" Brownley unveils a secret weapon to face the local tribes—and what follows is chaos only two mountain men could walk into by accident.

This two-book bundle includes the thirteenth and fourteenth novels in the Uzziah Mountain Man Series.

AVAILABLE FEBRUARY 2026

ABOUT THE AUTHORS

He was good looking and could sell ice to eskimos. But ... writing asked something else from him. He would have to corral his interest in being free. Writing would take him to a place where he was tamed, but also able to actually tell a story.

After the first two weeks at the Yale School of Drama, he called the head of the playwriting department, Milan Stitt and told him he was quitting. Milan invited him to lunch at a nearby Mexican restaurant in New Haven. He told the man who had had plays on Broadway that he wanted to be a free writer. Milan smiled, then explained the way to freedom was always through discipline.

Something in him clicked and it all began to make sense.

Three years later, when he received his MFA in playwriting, he received the much coveted Cole Porter Prize for Excellence in Writing.

Enter a woman, years later, when the first 'J' in J.J. Bonham, Jack Bonham, had written thirty screenplays in 7 years and had one optioned which looked like it actually might be done.

Unlike Milan Stitt, this woman had no plays on Broadway, but was a divorced mother of four grown children. She loved soaps, and was an ardent watcher of the same. In the years of her devotion to watching she developed an uncanny ability to discern plot and analyze character. Uncanny, really better than any of his teachers at Yale.

They, Jack & Judy, the other 'J' in J.J. Bonham, married in Buffalo Springs, Colorado. While teaching elementary school in Denver they read the same novella and looking up and into each other's eyes, realizing something. They could do that.

Thirteen years later they had written nearly 200 novels. Westerns mostly because that was who they were – a misplaced couple from the 19th Century who saw life in a western justice sort of way. They danced in Virgina City, Montana. Dances from a different time and place, but still their time and place.

Now, they live in the Bitterroot Valley on five acres and looking out the office window as he puts this together for them, he can see the thunderstorm marching across the Sapphire Mountains. Earlier, sitting on the porch, she had said something about the crack of lightning years before as they said vows of love in Buffalo Springs. He remembered.

www.ingramcontent.com/pod-product-compliance
Lightning Source LLC
La Vergne TN
LVHW041250110826
845146LV00005BA/1332

* 9 7 9 8 8 9 5 6 7 8 0 3 9 *